"I have an announcement to make of particular interest to first year students, or should I say to one first year student in particular." Madame Preston looked around the room, her eyes resting on Kay for a moment. "As you all know, Ballet Canada will be opening at the War Memorial Opera House next week."

An excited murmur rippled through the room.

"The Bay Area Ballet Company is currently having quite a successful European tour, and their engagement abroad has been extended for another two weeks. Usually when a visiting company comes to town, they need to fill in a few spots in the corps. Bay Area Ballet apprentices and younger corps members generally get the job, but since we're a bit short right now, all of you are going to get a chance to appear with this major company."

From the back of the room Katrina Gray voiced everyone's surprise. "We're actually going to be on stage with Ballet Canada?"

"On stage with Lynne Vreeland!" Leah and Alex said in unison, turning to tease Kay. She was standing with her hands clasped tightly in front of her, staring at Madame as if she had seen a ghost.

STARS IN HER EYES
Satin Slippers #3

Elizabeth Bernard

FAWCETT GIRLS ONLY • NEW YORK

RLI: $\underline{\text{VL 7 \& up}}$
      IL 8 & up

A Fawcett Girls Only Book
Published by Ballantine Books
Copyright © 1987 by Cloverdale Press, Inc.

Library of Congress Catalog Card Number: 87-91007

ISBN 0-449-13302-8

Manufactured in the United States of America

First Edition: February 1988

With special thanks to Freed of London, K.D. Dids, and
Baryshnikov Bodywear by Marika.

To Kevin and Carmen

Chapter 1

November dawned rainy and cold and Leah Stephenson awoke to the sound of fog horns bleating through her bedroom window. She opened her deep blue eyes and was greeted by the sight of a generous bouquet of pink and magenta peonies cascading out of an old orange juice jar. Before going to sleep the night before, she had put them on the low wicker table near her bed so their delicate fragrance would scent her dreams.

She sighed and rolled over on her back. Her long blond hair fanned out on the pillow and she absently combed her fingers through the silky tangles. The steady drum of the rain on the roof was hypnotic, and Leah stared at the ceiling, fighting against sleep and trying to remember the dream she'd been having.

She was wearing a tutu the same vivid pink as the peonies. She couldn't remember what ballet it had been, but she was the star, and as the final curtain fell, the audience broke into tumultuous applause. A woman rushed in from the wings and gently patted her face with a towel. Kind hands helped her fix her hair. Then someone held the curtain open and she stepped out onto the apron of the stage and sank into a deep gracious bow. It wasn't the stage of the San Francisco Ballet Academy auditorium, where Leah went to school. The grand and gilded proscenium was that of an opera house Leah had never been to. The crowd roared louder and from the balconies thousands of flowers pelted her like rain. Then her partner took her hand and helped her to her feet. Leah scooped an enormous peony off the floor of the stage and handed it to him, raising her eyes to meet his. Only then did she notice it was James.

"James Cummings!" Leah said, bolting up in her bed. Well, this was one dream that wouldn't come true. She got up and put on her terry-cloth robe, tying the belt tight against the cold. Of course, dreaming of her ex-partner made perfect sense. The peonies on the table were from him. Leah's friend, Alexandra Sorokin, had invited him to a small gathering at the boardinghouse the night before, and he had presented Leah with the beautiful bouquet the minute he walked in the door. Seeing James again, even on crutches, for the first time since his accident had definitely cheered her up. And reading James's note later had made her feel better. Leah crouched down by the low table and fingered the card thoughtfully.

"Dear Leah," the card read.

I know this can't make up for the trouble I've caused you. You were right all along and I'm so

sorry things turned out this way. You really are
the best dancer I have ever worked with. Maybe
fate will throw us together again someday.

                                    Your friend,
                                    James

James's signature was a bold flourish that looked
more like an autograph. Leah had the feeling, just
from looking at it, that in spite of the obstacles
James would face, he was destined to be a star.
The thought relieved her. After his terrible fall
during their pas de deux at a local high school
dance demonstration, she was afraid he would
never dance again and she would have felt re-
sponsible. Madame Preston, the director of the
prestigious dance academy, had nearly blamed
her when she called her into the office the day
after the accident. It had been a sobering experience, mainly because Leah had had to face the
disappointment in her stern but beloved teacher's cool gray eyes. Until then, Leah had been her
favorite pupil. She left the interview knowing that
not stopping James from dancing on a serious
injury could have harmed her as much as it had
harmed James. Leah and James had been rehearsing together when he had hurt his ankle
badly. He had made Leah promise not to tell
anyone and had gone on dancing on his injury
until his terrible fall in front of an audience. Leah
knew now she should have told one of her teachers before the demonstration. She should never
have danced with him knowing he was hurt.
  As punishment she was grounded for a month,
unless Madame Preston shortened her sentence

when she returned from the company's European tour. Leah forced back the momentary wave of anger that swept over her. Because of James, her activities were limited to the Academy grounds and the boardinghouse proper. Because of James, she was going to miss out on Ballet Canada's West Coast tour and the nine performances scheduled next week at San Francisco's War Memorial Opera House. Because of James, she would not get to see Lynne Vreeland, Ballet Canada's biggest star, perform during what was to be her last season before retiring. For a moment Leah hated James. The next instant she was overwhelmed with guilt. James was hurt. She wasn't. James's future as a dancer, not hers, was in jeopardy. And James's punishment had been much more severe than hers. Madame Preston had kicked him out of school. Alex had taken a big chance inviting him to the boardinghouse that was run by Madame's sister, Mrs. Hanson.

Leah gently fingered a peony blossom, then grabbed her towel and a new bar of soap. Quietly she opened the door to her room and raced down the top floor hallway to the shower and back before any of the other girls boarding at Mrs. Hanson's had even gotten out of bed. She wriggled into her best jeans and walked over to the dresser.

A glossy Ballet Canada brochure lay open beneath her makeup case. Leah shoved it aside and pulled her fuzzy pink turtleneck over her head. Then she set to work on her hair. With quick deliberate strokes of her brush she had smoothed it back up and off the nape of her neck and within seconds had secured the thick blond waves into a tight bun.

She tried to clear her head of her distressing thoughts. Being upset about missing Lynne Vreeland's performances wouldn't help a thing, and neither would being late for Christopher Robson's morning class. With the company and Madame away, Christopher had taken over the girls' class. He was a guest instructor at the school this year, and a former partner of Leah's first ballet teacher, Hannah Greene. Leah found him stricter than Madame, and not as inspiring. He was particularly tough on her these days, probably because of that business with James. Being late for class today would just be begging for trouble. She glanced over at the big blue alarm clock beside her bed and saw it was already a quarter to nine. Without bothering to put on makeup or earrings, Leah grabbed her bright yellow slicker and hurried out the door of her top floor room. If she rushed, she'd just have enough time to pick up Kay Larkin, one of her best friends at the boardinghouse, and walk the quarter mile to the Academy.

She banged on Kay's door, then walked right in. Kay's half of the spacious double room looked even messier than usual. Kay's roommate, Melanie, was nowhere in sight. A fast-paced morning talk show was blaring on the radio. Leah winced when she finally noticed Kay standing in front of the full-length mirror on her closet door, wearing only a bra and pink tights. It was almost time for class and she wasn't even dressed yet. She waved at Leah's reflection and put one foot through her leotard.

Leah tried not to look annoyed. Ever since Kay

had heard about Ballet Canada's scheduled week of performances at the Opera House, she'd been acting a little strange. The prospect of seeing Lynne Vreeland, her favorite ballerina, in person for the first time seemed to have made her more unreliable than usual. Recently she'd been late for everything and unbelievably spacy. At the boardinghouse dining table the past few days she'd been too excited to eat. Leah eyed her friend critically. She was actually getting too skinny. Just as Leah was about to warn Kay not to drop too much weight, Kay shouted something Leah couldn't hear, than half hopped, half tripped over to the dresser and flicked the radio off. "Madame's back!" she announced, yanking the stretchy fabric of her leotard over her small round hips.

Leah whistled softly under her breath. She sat down heavily on the edge of Kay's unmade bed and stared at her friend. "I—I thought the company was on tour for two more weeks."

"It is," Kay replied, slipping her arms into the sleeves of her leotard and pulling on a tiny denim miniskirt. "After London and Paris they went on to Munich, or maybe Amsterdam. I don't remember which. But she must have left the company after the performances in Paris." Kay's smile turned into a concerned frown. "Leah, what's wrong? I thought you'd be thrilled. Now you can come to Ballet Canada with us. Ten to one you're free at last! Remember, Madame said you were grounded for a month or at least until she got back. It's been three weeks now and I'm sure all's forgiven and forgotten." Kay grinned broadly. Then added as an afterthought, "I bet the whole school gets comps to the Ballet Canada performance." She pirouetted gaily in front of the mirror, then let out a profound sigh. "I can't believe I'm actually going to get to see Lynne Vreeland." She clasped her hands in front of her and gave a nervous giggle. "I never have, you know, except on TV."

"I know, I know!" Leah moaned. "You've told me that ten thousand times over the past two weeks. I'm looking forward to seeing her, too," Leah went on grumpily, "but Ballet Canada's tour is certainly not *the* most important event in my life just now." Her voice caught and she quickly cleared her throat to cover up her uneasiness. For three weeks now she'd tried to keep her feelings to herself, but her fears about James and her own future at the school had been building up inside her. Suddenly Leah was sure she was going to cry, and she bent over to hide her face. With slow, deliberate movements she neatly tucked the bottoms of her stonewashed jeans into the tops of her purple rubber boots. "I'm ready for Ballet Canada," she said slowly, "but not for Madame Preston."

"You're upset because Madame's back!" Kay's eyes grew big with surprise.

"Yeah," Leah admitted reluctantly, straightening up now that her feelings were under control.

Kay instantly crossed the room to where Leah was sitting. "Oh, come on, Leah. Everything's going to be okay now," she said earnestly. "Madame isn't the type to hold a grudge."

"How you know?" Leah snapped, then snorted in disgust. "Listen to me!" She shook her blond head vehemently. "It's just, well, neither one of us knows Madame all that well. We've been here only two months. I don't know about you but—"

Leah broke off and propped her elbows on her knees, then stared bleakly out the window at the rain. "The longer I'm here at SFBA, the more I realize I don't know a thing about what really counts in the dance world. Look at James. One mistake and poof, his whole career's in question. He's only eighteen, Kay," Leah said emphatically. "I wasn't kicked out or anything, but what if Madame hates me now? I really feel like I let her down." Leah's voice wobbled on the last few words.

"Don't be a dope!" Kay scoffed. Her expression softened as she regarded Leah's sad face. "So that's what's been worrying you all these weeks." Kay crouched down beside Leah and looked up into her eyes. "You're too good a dancer for Madame to give you a hard time—"

"James is a *great* dancer—"

"James is a little crazy," Kay countered firmly. "And *he's* the one who insisted on dancing when he was injured. Besides, you have no idea what's going to happen to him." Kay cut herself off and quickly averted her glance from Leah.

Kay knew something about James. Leah could tell. Kay worked in the school's office part-time and was always the first to hear any exciting news. Leah was dying to hear what her friend knew and wondered exactly how to get it out of her. She decided the direct approach was best.

"Do *you?*" she asked. "Do you know what James is up to? Did you overhear something in the office that you haven't told me?"

Kay turned around and looked at Leah wide-eyed. "I didn't say I knew a thing."

Kay brushed her long, unruly hair away from her face with her hand and broke into a sheepish grin. She colored slightly and the light dusting of freckles across the bridge of her nose suddenly seemed more pronounced. She sat down next to Leah on the bed and let out a long sigh. "I shouldn't be telling you this," she warned, but her round blue eyes were sparkling with excitement. "And I didn't hear it in the school office either. I actually heard it from Alex and I sort of promised her I wouldn't tell. After all, it *is* her news."

Leah gave an impatient grunt and Kay went on quickly. "James talked to Alex last night!"

"Of course he talked to Alex!" Leah looked up at the ceiling. "He talked to me, too."

"And brought you flowers!" Kay reminded her with a mischievous glint in her eyes.

"They were just to apologize. He *did* get me into trouble, remember?" Leah said testily, willing herself not to blush. There had been nothing, absolutely nothing, between her and her partner except for one brief kiss. She could picture James so clearly now: his large dark eyes, black hair, and velvety good looks. When she had been chosen to dance as pas de deux from *Romeo and Juliet* with him for the initial round of dance demonstrations to be given in area high schools, Leah had been considered the luckiest girl at the Academy, although she hadn't been quite as convinced as everyone else about her good fortune. James's arrogance and haughty manner had put her off since her first brief encounter with him during audition week, before she was even accepted into the school. Actually dancing with James had changed her opinion of him. She had found herself hypnotized by the way they had moved so perfectly together, as if they were made for each other. As a partner he had been kind, considerate—and confusing. Each time the music stopped, James the gallant partner vanished and James the egotist appeared. But slowly he began to let down his guard. He had even asked her out to the museum once. Leah had actually started to like him, and the better she knew him, the more she wanted to know about him—until his injury. Forcing her to keep his secret from all the teachers in the school had been a pretty dirty trick. Leah was still angry at him for that.

"I don't even *need* three guesses to know who you're thinking about!" Kay's teasing voice jolted Leah back to the present. She brushed at an invisible speck of lint on her jeans and ignored Kay's taunt. After a second she addressed Kay a bit gruffly.

"Are you going to hurry up or what? I want to hear about James, but I don't want to be late for class."

Kay nodded vigorously and quickly brushed some blush on her cheeks. "Well, I guess Alex won't mind if I tell you. James is okay. He can't dance for another month yet, but the doctor says he'll be fine, *if* he comes back slowly."

"That's a big if!" Leah commented acidly.

"Yeah, well, maybe for the *old* James, but Alex thinks he's really changed. A new and improved version of his highness, James Cummings." Kay giggled wickedly.

"Spare me!" In spite of her own worries about Madame, Leah was pleased to hear the news. After a moment's laughter she faced Kay with a frown. "But where's he going to go from here?"

Kay paused for effect, then continued in a dramatic voice. "James is going to audition for the Joffrey. They're holding auditions this week in that studio building not far from the Opera House."

"What?" Leah gasped. "But you just said he can't dance yet."

"I know what I said." Kay checked her wristwatch and grabbed her brush from the night table. She pulled it through her tangled curls once, then tossed it aside and reached for a box full of hairpins. She talked more quickly now. "Melanie went to take an audition class this morning."

"I know, I know," Leah said impatiently.

"But since James can't dance just yet, he's sending the video tape of the *Bluebird Variation* he made with Alex last year. Melanie took Alex's copy with her this morning. On the phone they told James a tape would be really helpful at this point. If they like it, they'll invite him to New York to take company class."

"So he won't stay here." Leah felt a curious stab of disappointment. New York was 3,000 miles away. She'd probably never see James again. Her feelings for the handsome young dancer confused her. On the one hand, she resented his arrogance and the way he had threatened her when she wanted to help him, but on the other, dancing with him *had* been an extraordinary experience.

"Not if he's smart," Kay stated knowingly.

"I guess you're right," Leah admitted with reluctance. She drew in her breath, pursed her lips, and finally said, "That's the problem, you see. It all comes back to the impression you make on people. I had everything going for me until the incident with James, and now I don't know how

Madame will treat me. I'm not looking forward to this class, believe me."

"Oh, Leah, would you stop worrying. Madame isn't going to stay angry with you. She wasn't *angry* with you to begin with. She just wanted you to learn a lesson, and being grounded hasn't been so bad, has it?" Kay paused and stuffed a handful of hairpins between her lips. She continued to mumble as she struggled to work her wild hair into a reasonably neat braid. "In fact, it's no different than usual around here. What else do we get to do most of the time? We're too busy dancing or doing schoolwork to go anyplace but school and here. It's not as though you've missed a homecoming dance or anything."

"Don't remind me," Leah said with a tight laugh. She sometimes wondered if one afternoon at a museum with James was the only high school date she was destined to have. She had no time for boys, even if she should get suddenly interested in meeting lots of them. She glanced at her watch and stood up. "Hey, come on, we've got to get going."

Kay grunted her assent and jumped up. She poked her head in front of her dresser mirror, somehow knocking the framed picture of Lynne Vreeland off the cluttered dresser top.

"Ooooh!" she shrieked, and the hairpins tumbled out of her mouth onto the floor. She dropped her hand and her hair flew out in all directions like a dark halo around her small face.

"I'll get them." Leah dropped to her knees and with one hand began fishing hairpins out of the white shag rug. She scooped up the photograph and smiled with relief. The glass panel hadn't broken. She cleared a spot on the dresser and carefully set it down. It was a beautiful picture, one Kay had bought for a couple of dollars from a balletomane who took the evening adult beginner class at the Academy. Like Kay, the ballet fan was a Vreeland freak and had actually followed the internationally renowned star around the USA, Canada, and parts of Europe over the years, taking live-performance photos and selling them to fellow fans.

Leah loved the colorful photo and was thinking of ordering one for herself, but suddenly it was as if she had never seen it before. Something about the delicate dark-haired ballerina was so familiar. She was wearing a long chiffon skirt, and her hair was flowing down her back. Leah didn't know what ballet the photo was from. It wasn't one of the classics, but something modern. The ballerina's right leg was in a high extension to the front, and her head was way back. She looked so ecstatic. Suddenly Leah gaped at Kay.

"Did anyone ever tell you you *look* like Lynne Vreeland?" Leah's voice was full of wonder. "You've got the same curly dark hair and round blue eyes. She's taller than you, but the way she seems to move in this picture is the same way you—" Leah stopped in mid-sentence. "Kay? What's wrong?"

Kay had turned white as a ghost.

"Nothing, nothing's wrong," she said with uncharacteristic brusqueness. Just before Kay turned away, Leah got a glimpse of her cheeks going from white to scarlet. Kay gathered her curls in both her hands and yanked them together. Grabbing a rubber band, she secured her ponytail, then bunched it into a rather messy bun. "No one's ever told me that before," she suddenly exclaimed, jabbing the hairpins angrily into her scalp. "Besides," she said, making a dismal attempt at sounding lighthearted, "lots of people have dark hair and blue eyes."

Leah was momentarily confused by her friend's discomfort. If she were Lynne Vreeland's biggest fan, she was sure she would be flattered if someone said she looked like her. Then Leah grinned. "The resemblance isn't as strong when your hair's up, but you really do look like her. No wonder you like her so much."

She paused to see the effect her words were having on Kay. But Kay dove into the closet without a word and began tossing out one shoe after another. Leah arched her eyebrows and nodded her head. In a silly singsong voice she teased, "That's why you're so obsessed with her. I bet you can't wait to see her up close to check her out, to see if the resemblance is really as strong as it seems here!" She tapped the picture with her finger. She felt quite satisfied with herself for having gotten to the root of Kay's almost groupie-like devotion to the world-famous dancer. Last night at the party, at Alex's urging, Kay had passed around her thick scrapbook filled with clippings from every phase of the soon-to-retire ballerina's brilliant career.

Kay emerged from the closet at last, waving a pair of pink rubber-topped rainshoes in the air. "Here they are!" she said in a falsely triumphant voice.

Leah flashed a knowing grin and folded her arms across her chest. She twirled her purple umbrella around and around by its cord and said in a voice that defied Kay to deny it, "Tell me I'm right. You love her because you look like her!"

"Not a bad theory," Kay said, cool and curt.

Leah stood dumbfounded and studied her friend. In the two months she had known Kay, Leah had never heard her sound sarcastic. Kay refused to meet Leah's glance. After an awkward moment, Kay rubbed her fists into her eyes and ruefully shook her head from side to side.

"I'm sorry, Leah, I didn't mean to snap at you," she apologized, but she still didn't look Leah in the eye. "I've got a dumb headache. Probably the weather."

"Uh, yeah. The weather," Leah mumbled. Five minutes ago Kay had been the picture of health, her usually bubbly self. This headache had come on very suddenly. She gave her friend a sidelong glance. What had she said that got Kay so upset? She really hadn't been acting like herself lately.

Kay didn't leave Leah much more time to worry. "Lynne Vreeland is not the most important thing on either of our minds right now," she said with a brusque wave of her hand. She hitched her dance bag up on her shoulder and picked up her ruffled pink umbrella as she marched out the door. "Madame Preston is," she continued in a light voice. "Neither of us had better walk in late her first day back," she declared, almost sounding like her normal, carefree self.

Chapter 2

The slow tempo of a waltz filled the Red Studio and a low murmur of groans rippled through the room. For three weeks there'd been no bow at the end of Christopher's class, but Madame's classes always ended with the classical ballet bow, the grand reverence. Most of the kids hated it. Leah loved it. She loved pretending she was on stage, graciously acknowledging the applause of the audience, thanking them. Today she really put her whole heart into the bow because her audience was Madame, and it seemed the school director wasn't angry with her anymore. Leah wanted to run up to the teacher and throw her arms around her. When she had walked into class this morning and taken her place at the barre, Madame Preston had greeted her with the barest of smiles, but a smile nonetheless. Leah didn't know if her punishment was over, but at least the director of the school didn't seem to hold grudges, just as Kay had said.

Alicia Preston's voice suddenly rose over the sound of the piano. "Katherine Larkin! What do you think you're doing? In this class we always start our grand reverence to the right. No?"

To the left of Leah, Kay cringed. "I guess I got off on the wrong foot," Kay muttered.

If class had gone better than expected for Leah, it had turned into a complete disaster for Kay. Madame had been on her case the entire time. Leah wanted to think that Madame's absence from class for the past few weeks had just made Kay's usual mistakes more glaring. Ever since she had arrived at SFBA, Kay's bubbly good nature and natural brilliance as a dancer had made teachers overlook a lot of her carelessness in class. Kay often started off on the wrong foot, or added one too many or one too few turns in any given combination of steps. Her extraordinary speed and brilliant allegro work seemed to make up for her lack of attention to detail. For the past couple of weeks, Kay's performance in daily class had been sloppier than usual. At first Leah had thought it was because Madame hadn't been there, and Kay had just gotten a little lazy in Christopher's class. But now that Madame was back, Leah started to suspect that Kay's mind was on something other than her dancing.

Leah glanced sidelong at Kay and her heart went out to her friend. Kay's blue eyes were focused on her feet. She looked extremely embarrassed and uncomfortable as she tugged down the back of her leotard and studied the toe of her shoe as she dug it into the floor. The room was so quiet, it was as if all twenty girls had stopped breathing.

"What in the world are you thinking of?" Madame stared at Kay long and hard and finally gave a bewildered shake of her head.

"Lynne Vreeland, no doubt!" Pamela Hunter commented snidely under her breath, just loud enough for the teacher to hear. Everyone knew how Kay idolized the famous ballerina.

Leah drew in her breath, waiting for Madame to further reprimand her friend. Instead, the teacher surprised everyone by breaking into a smile.

"If that's the problem, Kay, I think I've got some good news for you. Something that might actually make you get down to work for a change!" She gave Kay an encouraging smile, and everyone relaxed. "But first," Madame continued, "let's go through the grand reverence one more time. To what direction do we begin?"

Kay grinned. "The right. We step to the right."

Madame turned to Robert, the accompanist, and asked him to take the whole waltz from the top. Leah watched Kay out of the corner of her eye and was pleased to see her perform the steps perfectly.

Madame then signaled that class was over, and the room burst into the customary round of applause for the teacher.

Clapping louder than anyone, Kay stepped up to Leah and murmured excitedly, "What do you think Madame meant? Will we get comps to Ballet Canada?"

"I don't know. I don't even know if I'm allowed to go yet. But that would be really great for you. House seats are much better than standing room."

Kay rolled her eyes up to the ceiling. "Leah," she scolded in a hoarse whisper, "I'm sure all is forgiven and forgotten. Madame certainly didn't act like she was mad at you. If she's mad at anyone, it's me. You're not the one who felt the heat today."

Alexandra Sorokin sidled up to the two girls and warned them, "If you do not shut up, things are going to get hotter still." She gestured toward the front of the room.

Meeting Alex's eyes, a smile flickered across Madame's taut lips. With a slight arch of her eyebrows she graciously inclined her head toward the students. She stood up from her stool and clasped her hands in front of her, making no move to leave the room. Instead, she waited until the clapping died down and the room fell silent. The girls exchanged puzzled glances. Usually Madame left directly after class.

"I have an announcement to make of particular interest to first-year students, or should I say to one first-year student in particular." She looked around the room, her eyes resting on Kay for a moment.

Kay grabbed Leah's arm and held on tight. Leah tried not to yelp.

Alex let out a low laugh. "Don't tell me SFBA's walking grapevine isn't in the know?" She looked at Kay, expecting some response. Kay shrugged. "You really don't know what's going on?" Alex asked, amazed.

"I don't hear *everything*!" Kay said with dignity, cracking a sheepish smile. For once she really didn't seem to know the latest gossip.

"If you guys would shut up, maybe Madame would actually tell us her big news!" Pam chided from behind them.

Alex turned around and looked at Pam. Then

with deliberate slowness she turned back to face
Madame. Leah envied the way Alex looked Madame right in the eye.

"As you all know, Ballet Canada will be opening
at the War Memorial Opera House next week."

An excited murmur rippled through the room.
Alexandra stood a little straighter and cocked her
head. Kay took a quick step backward. Leah
crossed her arms and waited. She wasn't sure if
any news about Ballet Canada really concerned
her, at least not until Madame suspended her
sentence.

Madame didn't shush the girls up. She waited
patiently for the flurry to die down.

"I know tickets will be scarce and expensive."
She paused, and Leah had the distinct impression
Madame enjoyed the mounting suspense.

"I would like to announce that every girl here
will get to see at least one performance."

"Free tickets!" Linda Howe whooped, then
clapped her hands over her mouth.

"Great!" Kay clapped and let out a laugh. Leah
met Alex's eyes. The two girls smiled and looked
at Kay.

"I knew that was what was bothering you this
morning. Wondering if there'd be any cheap seats
left," Alex said, giving Kay a playful nudge.

Madame Preston again waited for the noise in
the room to die down, then surprised everyone
by saying cheerfully, "Yes, some seats have been
reserved for students and staff, but I think some
of you might get to watch the ballet from an even
better vantage point!"

"I knew it!" Alex screeched and bounced up
and down on her toes.

"Of course, our old hands at the Academy might have figured this out already."

Everyone stared from Madame to Alex and back to Madame again.

The school director leaned back against the piano and paused to smooth a wrinkle out of the skirt of her pale pink suit. After an agonizing interval she looked up at the class and continued. "The Bay Area Ballet Company is currently having quite a successful European tour, and their engagement abroad has been extended for another two weeks. Usually when a visiting company comes to town, they need to fill in a few spots in the corps, and for major productions they always need some nondancing extras. Bay Area Ballet apprentices and younger corps members generally get the job, but since we're a bit short right now, each of you will get a chance to fill a walk-on role in one of the full-length ballet classics Ballet Canada will be performing. It's too bad this opportunity is coming up before our own holiday *Nutcracker,* when you'd all have a chance for walk-on and small dancing parts. This is plunging you right into the middle of things without— for some of you—any professional experience."

From the back of the room Katrina Gray voiced everyone's surprise. "We're actually going to get to *perform* with Ballet Canada?"

"On the same stage with Lynne Vreeland!" Leah and Alex said in unison and turned to tease Kay. She was standing with her hands clasped tightly in front of her, looking a little pale. She was staring at Madame as if she had seen a ghost.

"How—how will girls get picked for this?" Kay

asked in a small, hesitant voice. "And is—is Miss Vreeland in all the ballets?"

Leah forced herself to keep a straight face. Kay sounded so scared, as if she wouldn't survive if she didn't get picked. Or worse yet, would be assigned to a walk-on part only when Miss Vreeland wasn't performing.

"Madame said all of us, Kay. *All* of us!" Alex stressed, reaching over and tweaking Kay's messy topknot.

Kay reached up and not very gently pushed Alex's hand away. She took a couple of stiff steps to the side, separating herself from the other girls. She pressed her hands together until her knuckles turned white, waiting for Madame to answer her question.

"I don't know Miss Vreeland's schedule yet, although you can be sure she'll be dancing at least one *Sleeping Beauty* and one *Swan Lake.* Of course the extras will take part in all the performances, matinees and evenings. It's simply a matter of who fits into which costumes." The silver-haired teacher pulled a piece of paper out of her pocket and ran her finger down it as she spoke. "Ballet Canada is bringing *Sleeping Beauty* and *Swan Lake* as well as some less elaborate productions. But party guests and peasant extras are needed for the two Tchaikovsky works. There will also be at least two openings for dancing corps and third-year students will try out for those roles." Madame stopped and smiled at Alex. "You'll like that, Sorokin!"

Alex grinned like a cat, and though not a strand was out of place, she stroked her immaculately groomed straight dark hair away from her face.

Leah envied Alex at that moment. She was a third-year student. Surely she would get to actually dance with Ballet Canada. Leah sighed, wishing she had just one ounce of her Russian friend's confidence and poise.

Madame Preston reached behind her and pulled a stack of photocopied sheets out of a manila folder that was resting on the piano. She beckoned Leah to her side, and said with a smile, "Leah, could you please hand these schedules out." Leah just stood there a second, dying to ask Madame outright whether or not she was among the girls to be considered for walk-on roles.

When Leah didn't move, Madame frowned slightly. Then understanding softened the hard angles of her face. "And don't forget to take a schedule for yourself." Leah knew that was Madame's way of letting her know she wasn't grounded anymore. With a little luck, she'd get to stand around the stage when Lynne Vreeland was dancing.

Leah's worries evaporated and she was suddenly all smiles. "Oh, thank you, Madame!" she cried, barely able to keep herself from throwing her arms around Madame's neck and hugging her. It was all she could do not to skip around the room handing out the papers.

She saved the last two schedules for her friends. Coming back to their side of the room, she handed one to Alex, then looked around for Kay. She was surprised to find she wasn't there. She hadn't even gotten her schedule yet.

"Where's Kay?" Leah asked Alex.

Alex whirled around and scanned the room. "I guess she left. Hearing about Lynne Vreeland might have been, how do you say?" Alex fished for the right American idiom. "The last straw. Her feet haven't touched the ground since the Ballet Canada posters went up around town."

Before Leah could respond, Madame spoke up again in a quiet but commanding voice. "This will be an important learning experience for each and every one of you. You'd better be prepared to sit around and wait. It will undoubtedly be boring at times, but you must remember to keep your eyes, ears, and minds open. You can learn a lot from working alongside professionals in a company the caliber of Ballet Canada. And remember, this will be your last chance to see Lynne Vreeland performing. She'll be retiring after this tour. She is a great ballerina, and I think we all could learn a lot from her." Madame turned away, then added over her shoulder, "And by the way, you'll be paid for this. Not much, but I'm sure the ten dollars a performance will come in handy. The company arrives tomorrow, Friday, and you should all report to the Opera House sometime tomorrow for fittings. You'll find out then when the first rehearsal is to be held."

A chorus of cheers met Madame's final announcement. Suddenly Leah knew that in spite of the ups and downs of recent weeks, she wanted nothing more than to study at the San Francisco Ballet Academy. For the first time in a month she felt inspired. Alicia Preston was a very great teacher. She had said time and time again that a real dancer never stops learning. Leah had always taken her words with a grain of salt, thinking that such a great dancer and teacher had nothing new to learn. But now she could see that

Madame really meant it. Leah wished Kay had stuck around long enough to hear what Madame had said. Kay worshipped the ground Lynne Vreeland walked on, and Leah was sure that once Kay got to watch her favorite dancer hard at work so closely, her casual attitude toward her own dance career would turn around.

Making a mental note to find a way to gently tell her friend this over lunch, Leah headed for the dressing room.

Chapter 3

An hour later Leah hurried out of French class, slamming the door behind her. The bang resounded through the empty corridor of the school's modern academic wing and Leah winced. She stood stock-still, her face scrunched up, dreading the moment when Monsieur Vuillard would fly into the hall and yell at her. Accidentally slamming a door in a teacher's face when he had just given you a pretty heavy lecture *and* a double dose of irregular verbs to conjugate over the weekend wasn't exactly smart. Getting caught memorizing Ballet Canada's rehearsal schedule instead of filling in an endless number of blanks in her French workbook hadn't been very smart either. Across the aisle from Leah, Pam had been doing the same thing, but as far as Monsieur Vuillard was concerned, Pam could do no wrong. She had lived in France one year when she was ten, and the teacher loved her and her flawless accent. Monsieur Vuillard did not love Leah Stephenson. Leah's accent was, in the teacher's words, "abominably American." She detested memorizing dialogues and messed up at least half of every vocabulary test. Above all, she'd never been anywhere outside of California, let alone anywhere near France.

Last week the teacher had called her provincial. Leah hadn't even known what he meant. She had looked it up and blushed at Webster's definition: a person of restricted outlook lacking urban polish or refinement. In other words, a small-town girl. His remark had hit home. Lately Leah had been wondering how she'd ever become a real artist, or have any depth as a performer, when all she knew about was dance.

Leah waited a moment longer. When Monsieur Vuillard didn't burst out of the classroom fuming, she shrugged her shoulders and headed down the hall toward the stairs and the basement lunchroom.

Rain had driven most of the students inside for their noonday meal, and the cafeteria line snaked out into the hall almost to the foot of the stairs. The noise in the narrow corridor was deafening and Leah momentarily felt overwhelmed by the crowd and the general din. The lunch scene at SFBA was usually quieter than at other schools Leah had attended. The dance academy was small, and everyone had crazy personalized schedules of academic and dance classes as well as rehearsals. Seldom did everyone converge on the small lunchroom at once. She stood uncertainly on the bottom step wondering if she should just forget about eating and go to the library to tackle that formidable list of verbs she had to master by Monday. Once Ballet Canada's fittings and rehearsals started tomorrow, she was going to have precious little time for homework.

"Leah, over here!" Alex's distinctive accent carried over the noise of the crowd.

Leah craned her neck and spotted her friend's dark head just inside the cafeteria entrance. She hesitated only a moment, then squeezed her way down the line ahead of the other kids, apologies on her lips. But no one seemed to mind her barreling ahead. Snatches of conversation revealed everyone was in high spirits because of the news about Ballet Canada and the chance for SFBA students to appear on stage with one of the world's most renowned dance troupes.

Alex shoved a tray in Leah's hand and shouted into her ear. "Where've you been? We have character class in twenty minutes. I think I'd better skip Mr. Mom's lunch special today." She passed up the steaming pots of hot soup and stew and reached for a modest-sized fruit salad.

Leah looked longingly at the tureen of hot chicken soup. All day she'd been cold, but Alex was right. Thanks to Monsieur Vuillard, she had all but missed her lunch hour, and Mr. Momous, fondly dubbed "Mr. Mom" by several generations of SFBA students, was known for fairly heavy, very tasty soups. Not the thing to gulp down fast before trying to learn the Mazurka. Leah chose some yogurt with nuts and berries, and followed Alex to the cashier's table.

While they waited to pay, Alex turned to Leah. "So what kept you so long?"

"Vuillard!" Leah groaned and raised her eyebrows. "He's on my case again."

Alex flashed Leah a sympathetic look. Alex spoke French as well as her native Russian, and she had tried to coach Leah many times. They both knew foreign languages were not Leah's strong point. "Extra homework?"

"Again," Leah admitted ruefully. "And with even less time to do it. Those rehearsals start tomorrow. Raul's taking us to the Opera House in the school van right after Madame's morning class."

"Where's your other third?" a voice boomed as the two girls finally reached the cash register.

Leah looked up into the round, beefy face of the mustachioed Mr. Momous. A fringe of gray hair circled his otherwise bald head. "Hi, Mr. Momous. I don't know where Kay is. I haven't seen her since class this morning." As she spoke, Leah looked behind her. The lunch line was longer than before, but Kay was nowhere in sight.

Alex frowned and scanned the packed dining area. "I haven't seen her either. Usually I run into her after American history."

"Don't look at me!" Mr. Momous said, throwing his pudgy hands up in the air. "I haven't done away with her." Leah and Alex laughed, and the cafeteria manager continued. "I haven't seen her pass this way. It's not like little Ms. Larkin to skip a meal."

"He's got a point," Leah said, as she and Alex looked around for two empty seats.

Alex considered Leah carefully. "That's not true. She's been skipping meals left and right lately. She's getting too skinny."

"I've noticed." Leah wondered why Alex looked so worried. "Kay's just excited, Alex. You know she's a real groupie when it comes to Vreeland. The prospect of actually meeting her must have been too much for her today. I never even got to hand her a schedule." Leah motioned toward her bag, where two sheets of paper stuck out of her French textbook.

"Well, she'd better get her feet on the ground fast. Madame was pretty rough on her today, in case you didn't notice."

"Tell me about it!" Leah groaned. "I'm glad I wasn't in her shoes." Leah scanned the room again.

"There!" Alex elbowed Leah. "Katrina and Linda are over in the corner. They managed to save us a couple of places. There's even enough space for Kay if she does turn up."

"Oh, she'll turn up. Even if she's too excited to eat, she's not too excited to talk about Lynne Vreeland, unless I've got Kay figured out all wrong!"

"Is the great Leah Stephenson admitting she was wrong about something?" Linda smiled and pulled out a chair for Leah to sit down.

"Cut it out, Linda." Leah pretended to look hurt. "I'm wrong about lots of things. Just ask Madame, or Monsieur Vuillard or— "

"We were talking about Kay," Alex broke in, pulling the wrapper off her straw. "I think something's going on with her. She's been acting a little strange lately and she hasn't been around much." She poked her straw into a container of apple juice.

"She was in class this morning," Katrina reminded her, scraping the last morsel of cottage cheese out of a bowl on her tray.

Leah settled into her chair and said, "But she rushed out almost before it was even over."

Linda looked thoughtful. "She did? I didn't notice." When she saw everyone at the table look worried, Linda laughed. "I bet Kay just flipped out when she heard she was about to commence her professional dance career by sharing a stage with her all-time favorite ballerina."

Katrina paused, her spoon halfway to her mouth, her thin face twisted into a puzzled expression. "Come to think of it," she said slowly, "I don't quite remember how Kay reacted at all. In fact," Katrina continued thoughtfully, her high pale forehead wrinkling with concern, "I don't remember seeing Kay at all. I said something to Linda, then turned around, and Kay was gone. She did run out rather quickly."

Alex leaned forward on her elbows. "It's just not like Kay," she said with a firm shake of her head. "She doesn't vanish when she's excited about something."

Linda laughed heartily. "Tell me about it." The willowy black girl drew her long legs up under her on the chair and propped her chin on her knees. "Kay's usually all over the place, and I mean *all* over the place, when she's heard a piece of big news. And performing at the Opera House is big news, Lynne Vreeland or no Lynne Vreeland."

"Well, as I said, something's definitely wrong," Alex insisted.

"What's wrong, Alex?" a familiar voice drawled. Leah groaned under her breath when Pamela Hunter appeared at their table and focused her attention on fishing out the strawberries from the bottom of her bowl of fruit and yogurt. She and Pamela had started out as friends during audition week at SFBA until Pam had shown her true colors. Pam still hadn't forgiven Leah for being the winner of the coveted Golden Gate Scholarship, an award given only occasionally to entering students of exceptional promise. The only other student at SFBA who currently held one was Alex.

"Uh, hi, Pam," Katrina said without much enthusiasm.

"You all don't mind if I join you, do you?" Pam asked, tossing her head to get her mop of thick auburn hair off her face. She sat down without waiting for an answer, gingerly lifting Leah's bag off the chair and dumping it not very gently on the floor at her feet.

Leah glared at her for a second, then folded her arms across her chest and pointedly looked the other way. She studied the rain pelting the earth just outside the narrow ground-level basement windows. Pam Hunter was one of Leah's least favorite people at SFBA. Without really meaning to, she had found herself in the midst of an ongoing feud with the Atlanta girl. Pam was one of the most ambitious and ruthless students at the Academy. She was also an extremely talented dancer, and Leah had no idea why Pam regarded her as such a threat. But right from the start of audition week at the school, Pam had set out to prove to the world that she, not Leah, was the top dancer in the entering class. After befriending Leah the day they arrived at the school, she then stole her audition variation. Leah had felt betrayed and very hurt. Both girls were accepted into the school, but the prospect of spending the next three or four years dancing alongside Pam and living in the same boardinghouse with her was pretty unpleasant for Leah. In fact, the two girls had barely spoken during their first month together at the Academy. On the surface, things were a bit better between them these days. Ever since Leah's problems with Madame, Pam had toned down her act, and she was actually civil sometimes. Still, deep in her heart Leah didn't trust Pam, and neither did any of her friends.

Pam began to peel a hard-boiled egg. Her scarlet nail polish looked garish against the pure white shell. For a moment Leah watched, fascinated. Pam managed to make everything she did look very dramatic and slightly sinister. Leah shook her head to get rid of that thought, and turned her attention back to the conversation.

"You all were discussing Kay," Pam stated, her tone inviting anyone to fill her in on the previous discussion.

No one obliged, so Pam shrugged and continued, after nibbling at the white of her egg. "Poor Kay. She looked positively green this morning. Didn't you notice?"

"Green?" Alex furrowed her brow.

"She means sick." Leah supplied the Russian-born student with a quick explanation. Alex's English was very good, but sometimes American idioms confused her.

"She looked pretty healthy to me," Linda asserted.

Pam shrugged again. "Well, I'm no doctor, but you should have seen her after Madame's announcement. She looked as if she'd seen a ghost. If I didn't know poor little Kay just worshipped the ground that worn-out old dancer walked on, I'd say she was upset to learn we're all going to get to work with her."

"She's not poor little Kay," Leah corrected Pam sharply, then bit her tongue to keep herself from saying more. She had made a resolution not to dignify Pam's cutting remarks by arguing with her. She knew Pam positively thrived on conflict.

Alex obviously had made no such resolution. "I don't know what you're trying to imply about Kay, Pamela, but I'm sure she's fine. She's just been a bit edgy lately. I have no idea why, really. And I'm sure you don't."

"But I do," Pam snapped, meeting the challenge in Alex's voice without flinching.

Leah took a deep breath and put down her spoon. "Well, let's hear your theory," she said with remarkable smoothness.

"Kay's flipping out. The pressure's too much for her, I'd say." Pam leaned back in her chair and folded her arms across her chest. She looked like a doctor about to give a patient some very bad news. "You'd have to be blind not to see it. Ever since we found out about Ballet Canada coming to town during Lynne Vreeland's retirement tour, Kay's been, well, off the wall."

"You're exaggerating," Alex scoffed.

"Madame noticed today. Kay's been so bad in class the past couple of weeks, I'm surprised she didn't get kicked out of here. Actually, I take that back. I'm not surprised at all. She is everyone's pet."

"You're just jealous," Linda said bluntly.

Katrina nodded in agreement. "Besides, Kay's a very talented dancer. Even you have to admit that."

Pam gave a noncommittal shrug and set to squeezing some lemon on her salad.

Leah wanted to speak up, contradict Pam, and defend Kay, but she couldn't. Not honestly, at any rate. Just because she hated Pam's guts didn't mean Pam wasn't telling the truth, or part of the truth. Kay *had* been acting weird lately, and everyone had noticed it. The memory of her own encounter with Kay just before class that morning suddenly resurfaced. Kay had seemed unbelievably touchy about Lynne Vreeland, about looking like her. Leah shifted uncomfortably in her chair. Maybe Kay was tired of being called a groupie. Leah recalled a conversation with Pam the first night she came to the Academy to audition. Pam had put Kay down pretty brutally for being an obsessive ballet fan and accused her of trying to befriend Alex simply because her parents were famous Russian dancers who had defected.

Leah had tried to defend Kay even then. Kay couldn't help being the type who went overboard about things. It was her nature. She got caught up in whatever was at hand and went at it wholeheartedly. The only thing she didn't seem to throw herself into completely was her dancing. It was as if dancing were something she really wasn't sure she wanted. Leah pondered that thought for a minute, then dismissed it. More than anything in the world, Kay must want to become a dancer, otherwise she would never have tried for this school. Attending a dance school like SFBA meant practically giving up life as a normal teenager. Only someone very committed to dance would choose to do that. No, Kay's dancing, or even Madame's annoyance with her in class today wasn't the problem. The more Leah thought about it, the more she began to think Kay had vanished because she didn't want to hear everybody digging into her about what promised to be one of the highlights of her life.

Leah suddenly wished she hadn't taunted Kay that morning. She made a mental note to seek out her friend as soon as possible and apologize. Sometimes, Leah reflected, people took Kay's bubbly good nature too much for granted. Leah was just beginning to get to know Kay after their first couple of months at the school together, and she suspected that beneath Kay's cheerful exterior was a sensitive, deeply feeling girl.

"Well, none of us knows where Kay is or why she's skipped lunch, but I do know one thing, Pam. Lynne Vreeland is scarcely worn out." Alex's defense of the ballerina brought Leah's attention back to the current conversation.

"I wish I were that worn out myself," Linda commented, sighing deeply. "Did you see her in *Giselle* on public television last week?"

"I'd like to know exactly when that tape was made!" Pam gave an insinuating sniff.

"Last summer at the All-Canada Dance Festival," Alex said with authority. "My parents were there. They saw that performance live."

"She is retiring now, though," Katrina reminded everyone. "But that's all the more reason Kay should be especially excited. It's going to be something to see such a famous ballerina on her last tour."

Leah could only agree with that as she vowed to help put her friend at ease about the upcoming performances.

Chapter 4

On Friday morning Leah dressed in record time and bounded down to breakfast humming her own unrecognizable version of a theme from *Swan Lake*. Only when Pam looked up from her breakfast cereal and plugged her fingers into her ears did Leah stop her off-key serenade.

She made a face behind Pam's back as she poured herself a cup of coffee. Then she settled into an empty seat near Alex and looked around the dining room table. Quickly the smile faded from her face. Everyone looked so glum. Before she could ask what happened, Melanie Carlucci broke the bad news.

"Kay's sick," she said sadly. "She's got the flu. Mrs. Hanson said her temperature this morning was a hundred and two. She can't come to class or fittings or anything today."

Leah stared blankly at Kay's roommate. "I don't believe it!" She sank back in her chair and cradled the steaming cup in both her hands. "What rotten luck!" She looked up and met Alex's eyes.

"I feel really terrible about this." She should have known something was wrong when Kay went to bed early last night without talking to anyone.

"Imagine how Kay feels," Melanie said, reaching for a pitcher of milk. "You should have seen her this morning. I've never seen anyone look so miserable." She set down the blue and white jug sculpted in the shape of a cow and propped her chin in her hands. "Kay's really devastated. Nobody loves Lynne Vreeland as much as she does. I wish it were me who was sick instead of her."

Alex pursed her lips. "You're crazy, Melanie! You're lucky you didn't come down with this flu, too. If you had missed that tryout with the Joffrey yesterday, it would have been much more serious than missing a walk-on role with a visiting ballet company. Even if the ballerina in question is Lynne Vreeland." Alex turned to Leah and frowned. "Leah, what are you doing?"

Leah had put down her coffee and pushed her chair back from the table. She was standing in front of the fruit bowl, filling a plate with oranges and grapes. "I'm going upstairs to try to cheer up Kay. I read somewhere that if your mental attitude is good, you recover faster. She's just got to be all right by tomorrow or she'll miss the whole Ballet Canada run!" Leah paused to look around the table, trying to find something that would appeal to someone with a fever and the flu. She grabbed a couple of pieces of toast and marched toward the stairs.

"Where are you going, young lady?" Mrs. Hanson called after her.

Leah spun around. She tossed her thick blond braid off her shoulder and smiled uncertainly at the boardinghouse proprietress standing in the kitchen doorway. "Uh, to see Kay. I thought I'd bring her some breakfast."

"No, Leah, that's not such a good idea. Kay seems to be really sick and I don't want all of you catching whatever bug got her. I think we'd better let her rest for now."

After one last glance up the stairs, Leah reluctantly turned back toward the dining room. "Do you think she'll be okay?" Leah asked.

Mrs. Hanson smiled. "Of course she will. That girl's got enough spirit to cure a whole hospital ward full of the flu." Without waiting for Leah's next question, she added, "And I'm sure something can be arranged with the visiting company if she's more herself by tomorrow. I already phoned Alicia—" Mrs. Hanson caught herself, and gave an embarrassed shrug. Her usual practice was to call her sister by a more formal name in front of the students. Mrs. Hanson cleared her throat and continued. "And Madame Preston says that since Kay won't be involved in any actual dancing, she's sure that she'll be able to take part in some of next week's performances. So don't you worry your pretty little head about it." The landlady gave Leah's braid a friendly tug and steered her back toward the breakfast table.

Leah tried to smile. "Kay will be glad to hear she still has a chance to appear with the company next week." She pulled up the sagging straps of her overalls and returned to her seat. But as she poured granola into her bowl, she couldn't quite get her mind off of yesterday's headache, today's flu. They had come on so suddenly, and Kay was usually as healthy as a horse.

Later that morning, when the school van deposited fourteen first-year students at the War Memorial Opera House, Leah hung back. She stood with one foot on the running board of the big blue van and one on the pavement, staring at the brass letters spelling STAGE DOOR. For the first time in her life she was about to walk into a theater through the same door real performers used: not just members of the corps of famous companies, but the door great dancers had gone in and out of for as long as the Opera House had existed. Leah closed her eyes and opened them again, then gave herself a little pinch. She wasn't asleep. This was real. It was a small beginning, a tiny baby step, but a step nevertheless toward making her dream of becoming a professional dancer come true. She wanted to drink in the moment, savor it, make it last.

"What's the matter, Leah? Did you put on two left toe shoes this morning?" Raul Zamora's joke interrupted Leah's trance.

She laughed in confusion and looked up blushing into the friendly face of SFBA's driver, fencing teacher, and drama coach. "Oh, Raul, it's just so exciting to be at the very beginning of something you've always dreamed of doing."

Raul's face lit up with comprehension. He gave Leah's hand a squeeze and guided her toward the door. "I know what you mean." He studied Leah intently. "And for you, young lady, it's certainly just a beginning. I think you are going to be one of those dancers who will be no stranger to concert halls more famous than this one."

Raul's compliment took Leah by surprise. She

liked Raul, but had never been as close to him as Kay and didn't realize he knew anything about her dancing. Before she could thank him, he flung open the stage door and ushered her in with a dramatic bow. "Good luck!" he called out with a cheerful wink, then turned and climbed back into the van. A moment later he was gone.

Leah took a deep breath and poked her head farther into the hall. To her surprise the back-stage entrance was rather grimy and small. The walls seemed to reek of old cigars, and a clumsy bulletin board littered with out-of-date notices met her inquiring eyes. Leah looked around, hoping someone would turn up to tell her where to go.

"What are you doing here?" a man's voice barked into her ear.

Leah jumped, and looked up into the eyes of an impossibly tall security guard. The sleeves of his steel-gray uniform were short, and he looked more like a forward for the Los Angeles Lakers than the employee of a world-renowned opera house.

"I—I'm here for a fitting," Leah said with a gulp.

"Your name?" His beady eyes were the coldest shade of blue.

"Stephenson. Leah Stephenson." Leah found herself speaking in the same staccato fashion as the guard. She lifted her dance bag from one shoulder to the other and impatiently tapped her foot against the linoleum floor.

The guard ran a bony finger down a soiled handwritten list. He read aloud with agonizing slowness. "Lord, Picchi, Stephenson." He looked up from the paper and down at Leah. "That way!"

He pointed down a narrow, poorly lit hall. "First left, second right. Follow the noise all the way." He threw his head back and gave a rather unconvincing version of a laugh, then seemed to fold himself in half and sit down heavily on a low stool to open up his newspaper.

Still wondering what the joke was, Leah pushed her dance bag higher up on her shoulder and ran down the hall repeating to herself, "First left, second right ... first left, second right." She wasn't sure what he meant about following the noise until after the second right. Even before she spotted the hastily printed "Wardrobe" sign with an arrow underneath, Leah figured out where the costumes were kept. No dancers were in sight, but from an open door at the end of the corridor she heard a chorus of voices and high-pitched laughter. She quickened her step and slipped into the room, hoping she wasn't too late to get a good costume. While she was outside the stage door dreaming of her brilliant career, all the other girls had gone on ahead to try on dresses. Would any good costumes be left? Roles would be assigned by who fit what costume.

She stood in the doorway trying to take in the confusion that met her eyes. She had expected the fitting schedule to be hectic, but she had thought it would involve just first-year students. Alex and the other candidates for the corps positions weren't due at the Opera House until later that day. The chosen ones would go right on to afternoon rehearsals with the company. But it seemed to Leah that all of Ballet Canada and its luggage was squeezed into the narrow space. The wardrobe room was bigger than a closet, but not much. At least thirty girls in various stages of undress were talking all at once. A dancer wearing a short white tutu brushed by her. Feathers fluttered off the tulle overskirt, then, caught in an invisible updraft, wafted into the air above Leah's head.

"Theees eeeze wrong, all wrong! Thees has my name, yes, but it eeeze not mine," the dancer cried with a pronounced French accent. Leah let her fingers graze the luxurious outfit as the French girl marched back in the other direction. To dance in a corps wearing something so beautiful would be heaven, she thought, and for a moment she once more envied Alex her chance to be a Ballet Canada swan.

"And you're ...?" A brisk but not unkind voice spoke up from over her shoulder.

Leah whirled around and faced a well-dressed blond woman in heels, a silky beige blouse, and wrinkled linen shirt. She was holding a clipboard and her eyes were bright and alert as they peered at Leah over tortoiseshell glasses.

"Stephenson," Leah said shyly. "Leah, that is."

The woman smiled, then quickly checked her list. "You're five four, are you?" She spoke with a crisp British accent. As she talked she took Leah by the elbow and gently maneuvered her over to a corner. "You can get out of your clothes here. Your bag will be quite safe, I assure you. Then go right over to Sylvie, our wardrobe mistress, and she'll see what we have that will suit you, not that you'll be much trouble." Again she appraised Leah as Leah peeled off her overalls and leotard and stood shivering in her tights and bra.

"By the way, love, if you need me, my name is Barbara Bartlett."

Feeling a little self-conscious in the roomful of strangers, Leah flashed Barbara a shy smile and made her way to a small, trim woman with a pincushion on her wrist. She waited while the wardrobe mistress helped someone out of an incredibly fragile-looking costume. It was a fanciful dress that seemed to borrow from all periods and Leah spotted it as being from the company's controversial new production of *Sleeping Beauty.*

"Now, *chérie,* this is too big for you, but we have another smaller version of the same thing. It is a muted blue and will suit you even better."

Leah was astonished to see Katrina emerge from the voluminous folds of rose brocade. Katrina grinned at Leah. Madame had given explicit instructions that morning that each girl was to look her best. Already Katrina's frizzy brown hair had come undone and was sticking out every which way. She had also lost an earring. "Everything's swimming on me. Imagine Kay!" Leah rolled her eyes. Katrina was slight, just under one hundred pounds, but about Leah's height. Kay was just five feet.

"Maybe it's best she isn't here," Leah reflected. Kay would die if she didn't fit into anything and had to miss performing with Miss Vreeland just because she was short.

"Is that the little one from the Academy who eeze so sick?" Sylvie asked Katrina as she expertly shook out a blue gown that had been lying in a trunk marked with mysterious initials: BC SB PROLOGUE. "Madame Preston gave explicit instructions to save something for her."

Katrina nodded. "She's really tiny." Her voice was muffled as Sylvie unceremoniously dropped the gown over Katrina's head.

"Don't worry about your friend. We have some tiny costumes," the wardrobe mistress went on. "For the wedding scene we need two small girls. You'll do for one, and this Kay, she can be another. We have back home a girl who is under five feet. She is a great dancer, too. She will be a soloist soon."

Katrina poked her head out of the gown and Sylvie stooped to zip her up. Then she stepped back and studied the costume. She shouted a few commands at the girl from Vermont. "Arms up, now curtsy, now cross your arms in front of you— so—and in back, like this." She kept her eyes glued on Katrina as she went through the motions. "Not bad!" she finally said, then pulled Katrina closer. With a few deft motions of her hand she had pinned in the couple of inches of excess fabric at the waist. "Now go over there to Madame Joelle and she will baste you in, label the costume, and you will be all set for dress rehearsal Sunday, okay?"

She turned around and looked at Leah for the first time. She tilted her head and considered Leah's body. "Try this," she said, handing Leah the rose-colored gown she had taken from Katrina. Leah slipped it over her head. The stiff material of the bodice felt prickly against her bare skin. She held her breath as Sylvie zipped up the back. The wardrobe mistress didn't step back to study her. "Take a look," she said with a note of pride in her voice. The angular French woman made space for Leah at the mirror. Leah stared at her reflection a moment before realizing the slender young lady-in-waiting looking back at her from the mirror was herself. The costume was a dream.

The tight brocade bodice fit her like a second skin and the soft rose color brought out the pink in her cheeks and deepened the blue of her eyes. As Sylvie fussed with the puffed top of the sleeves, Leah made herself stand taller. She hadn't even seen the ballet yet, but already she felt like a true lady of the court. When she first entered the wardrobe room, Leah had felt disappointed she wouldn't be wearing a white swan's tutu. But now, dressed as a noblewoman from a fairy-tale kingdom, she felt the part with every inch of her body. She turned her head and craned her neck to see the back of the satin-bustled skirt.

Sylvie considered the effect carefully. Brushing her straight hennaed bangs out of her dark eyes, she let out a hearty, "*Bon!* You carry yourself like the blood relative of a princess! For you it is natural! Wear it well!" She turned around and hurried to a knot of corps girls arguing hotly about some mixup with their costumes. Leah wasn't sure if she should see Madame Joelle, as her dress didn't need basting, but it surely needed a label. She lined up behind Katrina and waited her turn.

A few minutes later she and Katrina were dressed again and out in the hall. "Do we have to go straight back to school?" Katrina asked in a loud whisper.

Leah was about to say yes, then looked around. In the time they had spent in wardrobe, the backstage area had begun to fill up. Up and down the narrow hall, dressing room doors were open and dancers in practice clothes were bustling between them. "Is the company rehearsing now?" Before Katrina could answer, Leah was digging in her bag for her schedule. "There's a men's class down in the A Studio—wherever that is."

"Let's check it out. Martin Thompson is guesting with the company this year. I'd love to see him in class. I don't think the men in the company are taking class with Madame, so this will be our only chance."

The girls looked first to the right, then the left. "Which way to the A Studio?" Leah whispered.

"I don't know," Katrina whispered back. "But we'd better look like we belong here. No one said we had to leave right away, but I have a feeling we're supposed to."

"Lost?" a friendly-looking ballerina asked as she paused outside a dressing room. It was marked with just one star. Whoever she was, she was a principal with the company. Leah gulped, hoping she and Katrina wouldn't get kicked out.

Katrina looked from Leah to the ballerina back to Leah again, panic written all over her thin face.

Leah decided to take a chance. She hoped her accent didn't sound too American. "Uh, yes. Where are the rehearsal studios?"

To her surprise the dancer didn't frown, look suspicious, or tell them to get lost. She didn't even call that awful security guard to boot them out. "This place is a bit of a muddle, isn't it?" she said confidentially. She proceeded to give them directions, then ducked back into her dressing room.

Downstairs most of the rehearsal studios were dark. The strains of a familiar Chopin étude filtered out of one of the large rooms farther down the passageway. "There!" Katrina pointed and quickened her pace. "And all the doors have windows in them. We'll be able to see just fine," she whispered over her shoulder.

Leah nodded and started to follow, then she gasped aloud. Not every studio was empty and dark, as she had thought. In a small room barely big enough for a piano and two or three people to rehearse, a woman was dancing alone in front of the mirror. "Katrina!" Leah cried in a hoarse whisper. "Come back here!"

Katrina walked back reluctantly, then whistled under her breath. "It can't be!" she cried, putting her hands over her mouth.

"But it is!" Leah was sure of it. There was no mistaking that carriage, or the incredibly soft port de bras and milky quality of movement. It was Lynne Vreeland. The woman in front of the mirror dancing to the tinny strains of Tchaikovsky issuing from a tape recorder on top of the piano did not look like an internationally famous star, but Leah knew that she was one. She looked slightly disheveled, but at the same time, to Leah's eye at least, wonderful. Leah would give anything to look as dramatically beautiful as that. Lynne Vreeland's thick curly hair was bunching out of her bun. An ugly pea-green scarf was wrapped in a careless turban wrapped around her head, and it matched the ballerina's moth-eaten leg warmers perfectly. The lacy trim of her black bra was showing above her low cut tank-top leotard. But in spite of her ill-matched outfit, she looked radiant. Her huge blue eyes were focused on her reflection in the mirror as she performed a series of arabesques and exquisitely slow attitude turns. Her control was incredible. She filled the space with star quality. Leah clasped her hands in front of her and watched spellbound.

"Wait until Kay hears about this!" Katrina said, turning to Leah with shining eyes. "Isn't she just wonderful? And doesn't she look just awful?" Katrina started giggling, and Leah clapped her hand over her mouth and joined in.

Between bouts of giggles, she stammered, "Imagine what her fans would think if they could see the glamorous Lynne Vreeland." Leah shook her head. "But seeing her like this is the most wonderful thing that's ever happened to me. She doesn't need costumes to make real magic!"

Katrina agreed wholeheartedly.

"What are you girls doing here?"

Leah jumped. It was the guard from the stage door. "Uh—we—" She looked helplessly toward Katrina.

Katrina gulped. "We're working with the company." The guard looked skeptical. He looked back at Leah and a dim look of recognition crossed his face.

"Oh, yes, I remember you. You two are from that dance school. You don't belong here today. Practice space is off limits except for company members. Now, go away, or I won't let you backstage again."

The girls grabbed their sweaters and bags and tore down the hall as fast as they could go.

Chapter 5

"*Ta-dah dah-dah—dah-dah!*" *Leah* bellowed an off-key flourish as Alex pushed open the door to Kay's bedroom. Melanie's portable TV was turned on to *Jeopardy*. The volume was up, very loud. Kay didn't turn her head or notice her friends' carefully choreographed entrance.

Alex raised her eyebrows and marched right over to the small red plastic set and flipped it off.

Kay's mouth fell open and she glared at Alex. "What are you doing?" she shouted, sounding to Leah like her usual boisterous self. "I was just about to win. What famous celebrity made a leap to freedom in 1961 in the romantic city of Paris?"

"Nureyev!" Leah, Alex, and Kay shouted all at once, then burst out laughing. Leah set down a dinner tray on the one clear spot in the middle of Kay's messy desk to the right of her bed. At the sight of food, Kay's face lit up. She swung her legs out of bed and tugged her red flannel nightgown down over her knees. "I'm starved!" she said, then catching the surprised expression on her friends' faces, she added quickly, "My fever's all gone."

Leah nodded. "We heard. We were all so afraid you'd miss out on Ballet Canada and Vreeland and everything." Leah flopped down on the bed as Kay pulled up a chair and dug into her salad. She munched a few minutes in silence.

Alex cleared her throat and said, "We've got good news for you."

"What is it?" Kay inquired curiously. She gulped down some milk and folded her hands primly in her lap.

"They're saving you a costume," Leah stated, smiling broadly.

"Whaaat?" Kay looked from Alex to Leah then down at her plate. She poked a hole in the small mound of rice beside her chicken. "You can't be serious. How could they do that? They don't even know my size."

Leah studied her friend. "You don't sound very happy about it. I thought you'd be thrilled. You'll get to be onstage like the rest of us now."

"Apparently rumors that SFBA was training the world's shortest ballerina have spread far and wide. You're already a legend in Canada," Alex said in her characteristically dramatic way. "Sylvie, the wardrobe mistress, is dying to meet you." Her shrewd eyes were on Kay's face.

Kay managed a smile. "I am happy about it. But I don't know if I'm well enough to actually dance."

Leah suddenly understood Kay's concern. "Oh, Kay, but you won't be dancing. Don't you remember what Madame said? First-year students just get walk-on roles. And you're certainly well enough to walk." She paused and hugged herself in delight. "You won't believe the costumes the court ladies get to wear in the prologue to *Sleeping*

Beauty. And Sylvie is saving you something from the last act. It's bound to be all gold and glamorous."

Kay toyed with her food. Her ravenous appetite seemed to have disappeared. "That's good, then," she said without much conviction. She looked down at her plate and wrinkled her nose. "I think my eyes were bigger than my stomach. I shouldn't have eaten my salad first. I'm feeling a bit woozy again."

"You just got up too fast. You're probably still weak. That was a very high fever," Alex said, helping Kay back to bed.

"Yes, that must be it. I *am* better. I don't have any fever now."

Leah thought she must have imagined it, but Kay almost sounded let down about her fever being gone. She considered her friend carefully. Kay seemed fine, just a little nervous. Leah gave an emphatic shake of her head. She kept getting a feeling that something was wrong with Kay, not the flu, but something two aspirins and sleep couldn't cure.

Kay sat up in bed and gave her pillows an energetic punch. She bounced up and down a little on the mattress, then reached for a tissue and made a big production out of blowing her nose.

"What *is* she like?" she asked out of the blue.

Leah noticed how cautiously her friend spoke. Usually she talked nonstop and very fast, never pausing to consider what she said, her words just tumbling all over each other in a rush. Tonight it was as if she were being extra careful. Leah looked at her friend puzzled, but when Kay caught her staring, she averted her eyes, and Leah wanted to kick herself. She had come up here to make Kay feel better, not to analyze her.

Alex spoke up first. "I can't imagine who you're talking about? Can you?" Alex turned toward Leah and winked.

But Leah wasn't going to play along. She had teased Kay enough about Lynne Vreeland, so her answer was straightforward. "Lynne Vreeland's— well—" Leah searched for the right words. It was so hard to describe the quality she'd seen that afternoon. "She's a real star, Kay."

Kay nodded slowly. "I suspected that."

"But it's so strange to see it in person, when she isn't on stage, and there's no makeup, no lights." Leah shivered at the memory, then recounted her experience seeing the ballerina rehearse that afternoon. "Katrina felt the same way I did. The magic comes from inside her. It was really wonderful to watch. I'm sorry you couldn't be there."

"Me, too," Kay said softly. There was such incredible sadness in her voice, Leah thought her heart would break.

"Oh, Kay, you will see her. You'll be on stage with her," Leah cried.

"Better yet, you'll take class with her tomorrow!" Alex said.

"What?" both Leah and Kay exclaimed at once.

Leah started laughing. "Listen to me. I totally forgot about that. The girls from the company are taking Madame's nine-thirty class tomorrow. It never dawned on me Lynne Vreeland would actually be there in person." Leah jumped up from the bed and paced a few steps before speaking again.

"And Mrs. Hanson said you were well enough to come to that."

"I did tell her that earlier, didn't I?" Kay's voice trailed off. She bit her lip. "I said I wanted to get back to class fast."

"Now, don't tell me that you don't want to go to class because you'll look bad in front of your heroine," Alex chided Kay.

"Yes, that's it—that's why," Kay declared with force. She gave Leah a sheepish look. "As I've been told more than once recently, I am the original Vreeland groupie around here, and I hate to think how wobbly I'll look at the barre tomorrow. Just walking to the chair tonight made me dizzy. I can imagine how I'll be in class. I'd hate to have *anyone* see me that way."

Leah sat down again at the foot of Kay's bed and jammed her hands into her overall pockets. She rocked back and forth slowly, thinking. "I've got it. You go to class, you do a couple of pliés, some dégagés. Just a few," she added quickly, seeing the worried look on Kay's face. "Then you ask Madame if you can stop. She'll let you sit out the rest of the class and watch from the front."

"Great idea, Stephenson!" Alex congratulated her. "That way Kay doesn't even have to work up a sweat in front of her idol."

Kay agreed to Leah's plan. "I'm sure that will work out fine. But enough about me. Tell me exactly how it feels to actually get to dance with Ballet Canada, Alex."

Alex made a face. "If you can call taking five steps out of the wings, doing two bars worth of bourrées, then vanishing into the wings again dancing, I guess it's all right."

"I'd love to be doing that!" Leah sighed.

"Well, it's good practice," Alex admitted, "and I get fifteen dollars a performance for that as opposed to your ten for just standing around on stage looking pretty."

"I beg your pardon!" Leah pretended to look offended and winked in Kay's direction. But Kay was staring out the window into the fog and not paying any attention to Leah or Alex or their description of their exciting first day backstage at the Opera House.

Get a move on, Larkin! Leah wanted to scream. But she didn't. Kay's mood the next morning was weirder than ever. The bounce had gone out of her step, and she was literally dragging her feet the entire six blocks from Mrs. Hanson's to the Victorian mansion that housed the San Francisco Ballet Academy. She had on her oldest jeans and a worn-out sweater, and she hadn't even bothered to put her hair up. Her usually springy curls hung limply around her small face. She couldn't have looked worse if she'd tried.

To bridge the unnatural silence between them, Leah had been talking nonstop. Now she had run out of things to say. This was not, Leah reflected wryly, the usual scenario on the way to school. Alex was the dramatically silent type and Leah usually said little during the walk to morning class. Kay was always the one who monopolized the conversation. But not today. Leah was painfully aware she was carrying on a one-sided conversation as Kay walked next to her, preoccupied. She hadn't said one word since they left Mrs. Hanson's. Every few steps she stopped and looked around anxiously, as if she were waiting for something to happen. Her nerves were contagious. Leah began to look over her shoulder, too. All she could see was the parade of trolley wires, streetlamps, and buildings descending the hill behind them. She wondered if Kay's fever yesterday had somehow affected her brain. A few paces ahead, Katrina and Melanie were gossiping about the Joffrey auditions. Snatches of their conversation floated back through the clear morning air. Melanie had gotten a callback and things looked good for her. Apparently the Joffrey scout had been impressed with James's video, too. James would definitely be going to New York for an audition at the end of the year. Leah waited for Kay to make some comment about James's stroke of good luck. But Kay, for once, was speechless.

Leah racked her brain for something to get Kay going, get her mind off whatever was bothering her.

"After we left your room last night," Leah confided in a bright tone, "I called my mom. You won't believe this, but you're going to get to meet her." Leah paused, waiting for Kay to react.

When she didn't, Leah pursed her lips and let out an exasperated sigh. "Kay, you aren't even listening." That, at least, got a response.

"Yes, I am. Your mother's coming up from San Lorenzo. That should be nice, to see your mother and all." Kay's voice sounded strained.

"Not just my mom," Leah enthused, zipping up her denim jacket. A stiff breeze blew in from the bay as they rounded the corner toward the school. The sky was clear for once. No fog. No rain. Just pure blue with the tiniest puffs of clouds. Leah

felt vaguely annoyed with Kay for not even notic-
ing the unusually beautiful weather. Kay was always the first to gripe about the fog. Leah lifted
her face to catch the rays of the morning sun and
continued. "Chrissy's coming, too. Mom said she
had a client here in the city who could definitely
get them house seats. They can't stay overnight.
Mom will have to drive right back, but at least
they'll be here for one performance. Maybe she'll
take us all out afterward."

Leah's news fell on deaf ears. "Kay!" Leah finally cried, exasperated.

"Huh?" Kay replied, startled.

"Oh, forget it." With a brusque motion Leah
turned up her collar, shrugged her shoulders, and
hurried after the other girls. Melanie was already
inside the front door. Alex stood on the front
porch of the Academy waiting for Kay and Leah
to catch up. Leah urged Kay to hurry. "Come on,"
she said, calling back over her shoulder. "This is
no day to be late."

Kay didn't seem to hear. She continued at a
snail's pace, a spaced-out expression on her face.
Leah shook her head. At that moment Kay was a
million miles away from SFBA. The petite dark-
haired dancer was once again looking back over
her shoulder as she mounted the last couple of
steps.

"Hey, watch it!" Leah cried, but her warning
came a moment too late.

Kay tripped on the top step and fell flat on her
face with a startled cry. She lay there a moment,
not moving at all.

"Kay!" Alex screamed, and dropped down on
her knees beside her.

Kay propped herself up on one elbow and grimaced. "Oooh, my foot. It really hurts."

"Wiggle it!" Leah commanded in a shaky voice. A bell rang from inside the school. It was nine A.M. That meant just fifteen minutes left to change and warm up for class. Leah suddenly felt angry at her friend. Kay had been dawdling all morning, and now this. She forced herself not to say a word, though. Kay couldn't help having an accident.

"I *can* wiggle my toes," Kay said with a hopeful note in her voice. "But my ankle really hurts!" Her blue eyes met Leah's. Leah helped her sit up. Kay looked down at her ankle. She flexed it experimentally and let out a sharp cry. "I don't think I can walk on it. I think it's sprained."

Alex scrambled to her feet and hurried to the door, heading into the school. She waved into the dark foyer, where a small crowd had gathered. "Kenny, Michael, come here. Kay's hurt and we need help getting her inside!"

"What happened?" Kenny Rotolo was the first one out onto the porch. The boys were already changed for class.

"I tripped, I guess," Kay said softly. She looked up at her partner. He was only slightly taller than Kay, but he was strong and compact. He knelt down beside her and gently prodded her ankle and shin bone. Kay yelped with pain.

"Sorry," he said.

Kay shook her head. "I'm sorry, too. Just when we were getting those lifts right in pas de deux class. I hope I can dance again soon."

"Dance on it? You have to be able to dance on it. You'll miss all of Ballet Canada's performances and—"

"And they already saved me a costume," Kay interrupted with a sad laugh. Leaning heavily on Kenny's outstretched arm, she struggled to her feet. Her rosy face went pale as she inadvertently put weight on her injured foot. "That might be the least of my problems," she said, placing her left hand on Kenny's shoulder and reaching down to rub her left kneecap with her right. "I seem to have bruised my knee, too." For the first time since she fell, Kay sounded genuinely upset.

"You'll be fine," tall, soft-spoken Michael Litvak said soothingly. "Here, let me," he said to Kenny, and scooped Kay up in his arms. Kenny held open the door while Michael carried Kay through and down the foyer into the back hall toward the physical therapist's office. Leah grabbed Kay's dance bag, and Alex picked up her books. As they followed behind the boys, Alex put one hand on Leah's arm, restraining her.

Leah looked at Alex, a puzzled look on her face.

Alex put a finger to her lips. "Something's really wrong with Kay."

"She will dance again, won't she?" Leah asked in a hushed voice.

"Of course she will," Alex said a bit brusquely, "but not in time for Ballet Canada's performances." Alex turned the corner as the two boys and Kay disappeared into the therapist's office. She stopped in her tracks and stared directly at Leah. "Kay made sure of that."

"You think she fell on purpose?" Leah gasped. Even as the words came out of her mouth she knew Alex might be right.

"You bet. I don't think she meant to hurt her knee. That could be serious, you know. But we both know she's been acting strange ever since Madame announced that we'd be working with Ballet Canada. And I don't believe she was really sick yesterday either. I used to pull that old thermometer-under-the-heating-pad routine back in Leningrad whenever I didn't want to get involved in one of our endless number of school productions. They were compulsory there, you know. And if you were a top student and your parents were famous dancers with the Kirov, you had to be in every one of them."

Alex tugged her pure white sweatshirt down over her white leather skirt and said in a puzzled voice, "I don't see why Kay should be upset by Ballet Canada. It doesn't make sense. She should be the happiest person in the school. Instead—" She flashed a quick warning look at Leah as Kenny and Michael started back down the hall. "Kay needs her bag," Kenny said, walking up to Leah. "You two better get to class. Madame's not going to want her model students late for class today."

Leah was happy to hand Kay's bag over and end this disquieting conversation with Alex. She didn't want to face Kay right now. She wanted to think about Alex's suggestion that Kay was trying to avoid being within dancing distance of Lynne Vreeland and her company.

Chapter 6

"Predictable, isn't it?" Alex murmured as she scurried behind Leah to find a place at the barre. The airy Blue Studio was jammed, and four Ballet Canada latecomers hurried to the front of the room to fetch the portable barre.

Alex was referring to Pam. Of course she had managed to wheedle a place right behind Lynne Vreeland along the barre on the right hand side of the room. No wonder Pam had left the boardinghouse so early this morning, Leah thought. She had arrived in time to position herself perfectly. Every time the famous ballerina turned around at the barre, she'd have Pam's flawless technique to admire.

The music started and Leah pulled her weight up off her hips and legs and lengthened her graceful neck. As she sank into her first plié, she glanced into the mirror past her own reflection to that of Miss Vreeland.

Today, to Leah's relief, Vreeland looked the part of the poised glamorous artist that she was.

She studied every detail of the great dancer's makeup and dress. Apparently Miss Vreeland's respect for the teacher who headed SFBA's highly acclaimed faculty led her to turn up for class looking like a model ballet student rather than the funky rock star she had dressed like yesterday. An attractive fringe of bangs and curls framed her face, but the rest of her hair was pulled into a neat bun. The oversized hoop earrings she had worn the day before had been replaced by tiny diamond studs. Her fuchsia tank-top leotard brought out her dramatic coloring and no moth-eaten leg warmers obscured her perfectly shaped legs this morning as she performed the opening series of pliés.

How terrible for Kay to miss this, Leah thought as she watched. Leah still couldn't understand why Kay had balked at Leah's observation that she resembled the famous dancer. The similarities were even more apparent at this close range. Leah would give *anything* to look like her, but especially to *dance* like her. Her dancer's eye took in the shape of the ballerina's movement. Her body instinctively sought to copy the way Lynne Vreeland tilted her head, opened her arm in second position. Within moments she stopped envying the ballerina's dark hair and large expressive eyes altogether and longed only to someday dance exactly as she did.

Halfway through the centre work, Katrina gasped in a breathless voice, "I thought this was class, not a torture session!" While Katrina tried to catch her breath, Leah leaned against the barre and mopped her face with a towel.

"It is challenging," Alex commented softly as she patted her dark hair in place and borrowed Leah's towel. "You can't say she didn't warn us."

"But look at Pam!" Katrina wailed. "What I would give for technique like that!"

Leah turned around. The southern girl was in the third group of dancers traveling diagonally across the floor in a virtuoso series of jumps and midair turns. Pam was the only SFBA student in that lot who had managed to get through more than half the combination without a mistake. When she reached the front of the room she landed solidly with a stylish flourish, then quickly looked around. Leah followed her gaze. Pam was greedily eyeing Lynne Vreeland. When she spotted the dancer, her face fell in disappointment. The ballerina hadn't even seen Pam's bravura performance. She was whispering to another Ballet Canada member as the two women retied their shoes over by the rosin box.

Leah couldn't help but gloat a little at Pam's disappointment. She turned her attention back to Katrina. The pale-complected girl looked limp and suddenly despondent.

"When I see other people dancing like that, it makes me wonder why *I'm* here!" Katrina said wistfully.

Leah looked at the delicate girl and said earnestly, "Because you're a good dancer, a beautiful dancer. You're just not as strong as Pam. But you don't have to be strong to dance those steps. You just—" Leah searched her mind for the right words. "Well, you just have to feel the rhythm in your body. You have to find a way to make the steps make sense to you. You can't be an athlete like Pam, but you can be airy and light and buoyant like yourself." She encouraged Katrina with a smile, then said, "Watch me. First just get the steps down."

Leah lightly marked out the difficult combination. As the first group began going through the routine again, she grabbed Katrina's hand. "Here, let's do it behind them." Leah led the way, marking the steps, keeping one eye on Katrina. The last time they repeated the combination Katrina finally got it right.

Soon it was their turn to dance it full out. "Follow me," Leah whispered. She planted herself in front of Katrina and waited for the music to start. She counted the two introductory bars and began the series of jumps. In the mirror she glimpsed Katrina and smiled. Katrina's frizzy hair was in disarray, but she was sailing light as a feather through the combination. Her jump wasn't as strong as Pam's, but she seemed to float and hover above the ground like a cloud. When the girls finished and hurried off the floor to make room for the next group, Katrina caught Leah's hand. "I did it. I actually got through." With shining gray eyes she added, "Thanks to you!"

"No way. You were the one who danced it. I just helped you figure it out," Leah said firmly.

She congratulated Katrina with an encouraging wink, but Katrina was staring past Leah, her eyes open very wide. Puzzled, Leah whirled around. She found she was just inches from Lynne Vreeland. The older dancer was smiling at her. Leah reddened but managed a shy ghost of a smile in return. A moment later Miss Vreeland walked away to join the second group performing the combination for Madame Preston.

"She noticed you!" Katrina commented in a breathless voice, sinking back against the barre in a mock faint. She stared with admiration at Leah. "She saw what a good dancer you are," Katrina declared. "I might have gotten through the combination, but you really danced it, made it look like something."

Leah's heart was thumping. She was torn between wanting to hide and shouting for joy. She blushed with pleasure and met her embarrassed reflection in the mirror. She let out a giggle as she and Katrina hastened to the back of the room. "She really smiled at me, didn't she?"

Katrina nodded. "And she didn't even notice Pam!" she said in a smug whisper.

Leah cocked her head and looked at the older dancer. The ballerina was standing behind Madame, marking out the next combination of steps with fluttery motions of her hands. No, she hadn't noticed Pam, and Leah wondered why. Pam had danced the same steps even better than she had. Large dramatic jumps with tricky midair turns were Pam's strong point, not Leah's. But after a moment she gave up trying to figure out why she had attracted the famous dancer's attention. As her mother always said, don't look a gift horse in the mouth. And having Lynne Vreeland take note of her was a gift no ballet student in her right mind would question too deeply.

Later that morning Leah stood upstage at the War Memorial Opera House, one hand placed tentatively against a piece of scenery, the other resting lightly on the shoulder of a young gangly boy from Ballet Canada's corps. With all her might Leah was trying to ignore the itch near her left ear. Andrew Maxwell, Ballet Canada's ballet master, had warned the nondancing corps members that they were as important to the success of the performance as the stars themselves. They were to be "on" at all times. He told them every gesture, every smile, every tilt of their head would be observed by the audience, especially on opening night, when the performance was to be broadcast live on television. In other words, no scratching, sneezing, or talking.

"You can take a break now!" Andrew's assistant barked from somewhere in front of the darkened auditorium.

"Thank goodness!" Leah reached up and scratched furiously at her neck. A trail of sweat ran down the lowcut back of her leotard, and the cotton practice skirt she was wearing clung to the backs of her legs. "I never expected it to be so hot!" she complained loudly.

Her partner grinned. "This is new to you, then?" His deep voice and assured manner belied his slight build. "It's still kind of new to me, too. I just joined the corps this year." He stretched his arms up and started toward the wings, beckoning for Leah to follow him. "By the way, I'm Wayne and you're . . . ?"

"Leah."

"It's pretty boring, isn't it," he said.

Leah shook her head. "Not for me, I love it. It's hard standing still, but there's so much to watch."

She gazed wide-eyed at the stage. From her vantage point in the wings it looked completely different from the few times she had been to the Opera House and sat in the audience. Dancers in various practice outfits were warming up, using every available banister, table, chair, or piece of scenery for balance. Princess Aurora's friends were onstage rehearsing their variation with the company choreographer. As they pranced prettily in their practice tutus, a stagehand wearing earphones noisily hammered something into the floor a few feet behind them. The accompanying piano music was drowned out, but the girls danced on and the choreographer just shouted louder. Leah had never expected so much commotion. She was tired from having to stand so long in an uncomfortable position. She'd much rather be dancing, but she was far from bored.

"I'm running downstairs for some tea. Want something?" Wayne called back over his shoulder. "I'll be right back."

"No thanks," Leah said. Spreading her skirt under her, she sat down on a pile of sandbags heaped in a corner and watched, fascinated, as the rehearsal proceeded.

"Don't let your shoulders get cold. It's drafty back here."

Leah looked up. Lynne Vreeland was standing in front of her, a light sweater over the bodice of a dingy practice tutu, and a steamy cup of tea in her hand. She was still wearing her stud earrings, but violet eyeshadow coated her eyelids, her mascara was on a little too thickly, and she had that crazy green scarf wrapped around her head again.

"Want some?" she asked.

"Oh—no, thank you." Leah scrambled to her feet. She felt she should do something formal, like shake hands or bow. She'd never met a famous dancer face-to-face before. She shifted from one foot to another, and was painfully aware of a small hole in the sleeve of her old black leotard.

"How long have you been at the Academy?" Lynne Vreeland asked in a matter-of-fact voice.

"Oh, just a little while," Leah answered. Then, feeling she sounded too brusque, she amended, "I mean, just since September. I'm a first-year student." Her fingers toyed with the dull brown fabric of her skirt.

"So this is very new to you."

Leah nodded.

"Well, I'm serious about the drafts. They're terrible for the muscles." Lynne Vreeland bent over and set her teacup down on the floor safely behind the sandbags. "Speaking of muscles, I'd better warm up again," she said with a companionable laugh. "Curtis is almost finished rehearsing the corps, and I'm on next." She pulled off her sweater and handed it to Leah. "Put this on. Even onstage, there's a draft. Don't let the lights fool you. You aren't moving out there."

With a little wave good-bye she proceeded into the wings. Leah clutched the pink sequined sweater to her and watched as the star blocked out the commotion around her and single-mindedly began her own routine of pliés, dégagés, and loose swinging battements. *Wait until I tell Kay about this!* Leah thought, then whispered a little prayer that Kay would get better fast enough to at least meet Lynne Vreeland.

"Places, please!" a voice rang out a moment later. Leah hurried onto the stage, slipping her arms into the sleeves of the sweater as she went. It was a little small across her shoulders, and the lights felt warm as she assumed her position next to Wayne. But she wouldn't take it off even if she began to melt from the heat.

"Now, remember, lords and ladies of the court, look interested, curious about the sixteen-year-old princess. She's a pretty hot topic of conversation on the castle grapevine. She's turning sixteen, a marriageable age by fairy-tale standards. And there's always been this air of mystery about her because of the strange events that surrounded her christening. You haven't seen her in a long time, maybe not since that fateful day when Carabosse predicted her dire fate. Keep all this in mind. When she comes onstage, be amazed by her unusual grace and beauty. Remember, your job is to emote."

Wayne giggled beneath his breath. "How exactly do you look amazed at someone's grace," he said. "People don't care about all these dramatics in this kind of ballet. They just want to see dancing."

Leah didn't pay any attention. The music had begun, and remembering her instructions from an earlier run-through, she turned and looked eagerly toward the wings. A moment later Lynne Vreeland made her entrance. Looking amazed wasn't difficult for Leah. Backstage Leah had noticed little laugh lines around the ballerina's overly made up eyes, but onstage she moved as if she were truly just sixteen. Leah and Wayne exchanged staged smiles and pretended to whisper to other courtly couples around them. Wayne cracked a silly joke and Leah found herself really laughing. Then she held her breath as the star made her bow to the queen, her mother, and the king, her father, then curtsied to her cavaliers. A moment later Lynne Vreeland stepped onto the toe of one foot and began the difficult Rose Adagio.

Chapter 7

During the dinner break Leah grabbed a soda and stole away from the buffet table set up in the Opera House lobby. Her mind was too full of dance to think about sandwiches. The magic she had felt as she watched Lynne Vreeland become a fairy-tale princess was a precious, fragile thing she knew would vanish if she chatted to her friends. And anyway, she had a hollow feeling in her stomach every time she thought about Kay. Here she was, enjoying herself, still wearing Lynne Vreeland's sweater, while Kay was back home at Mrs. Hanson's in who-knew-what condition. Leah slipped into a hallway off the lobby through a side door.

The pay phones were a short way down the hall. Leah fished in the bottom of her dance bag for her change purse, pulled out a quarter, and put it in the slot. She hesitated before beginning to dial. Exactly what would she say to Kay? It more or less depended on how Kay was. If her injury wasn't as bad as it had looked this morning when the guys carried her to the therapist's office, then Leah would tell her everything, encouraging her to get back on her feet fast enough to get to at least one class with Lynne Vreeland present so she could meet her. Leah smiled. She could picture the ballerina being especially nice to Kay. A star like that would understand how let down Kay must feel, not being able to dance this week of all weeks. Lynne Vreeland had been young once. She must remember how important it was to meet the star of your dreams.

But if Kay was really hurt, and stuck in the boardinghouse for the duration of Ballet Canada's run ... Leah bit her lip and cut off that thought. No point worrying about problems before they come, as her mother liked to say. With a firm finger she punched out Mrs. Hanson's number and waited for someone to pick up.

"Hello?"

"Kay?" Leah gasped. "Is that you?"

"Sure. You don't see me for a couple of hours and you forget my voice?"

"Uh, Kay," Leah faltered, then went on. "You sound great. I expected you to be in bed, crying your eyes out. Which phone are you on? How's your foot, or your knee?" Kay sounded so good, it could only mean one thing.

"Oh." Kay's voice dropped. "Well—"

There was a moment's silence.

Leah leaned back against the concrete wall. The coldness of the stone penetrated the softness of Lynne Vreeland's sweater. "Kay, is it okay?" Leah finally asked. She held her breath. Leah pictured the phone in the boardinghouse. There were none upstairs except for private ones some girls had installed in their rooms. Kay had no phone in her room, so she must have been down-stairs. At least she could walk that far. The news couldn't be that bad. Just as Leah began to breathe again, Kay spoke up.

"Well, nothing's broken. The X-rays showed that," Kay said slowly. "But—"

"But what?" Leah knew Kay hadn't broken her leg. It wasn't that bad a fall.

"I can't dance on it," Kay stated simply.

"For how long?" Leah asked in a hushed, fright-ened voice. She grasped the metal phone wire tightly.

"I—I'm—well, Carolyn said at least not until it feels better." Carolyn was the school's physical therapist. Kay began speaking more quickly now. "That's exactly what she said."

"But what's wrong? Carolyn must have said," Leah pressed, feeling vaguely annoyed that Kay wasn't being specific enough.

"I don't know. I bruised my knee, and my ankle hurts. Probably a sprain, she said," Kay added hurriedly.

Leah slid her back down the wall and crouched on the floor. The phone cord barely reached. "So you don't know if you'll be well enough to come to class with the company or anything like that."

"No. But I don't think it's likely. Not likely at all." Kay's response was abrupt.

"I'm so sorry, Kay," Leah sprang back up to her feet and pressed her forehead against the wall. "Maybe you can get to a performance or two." Leah forced herself to sound cheerful. "In fact," she said a little too brightly, "I bet Madame will save some of those comps for you. Raul will drive you down and all that—"

"I don't know."

"You don't know what?"

"About that. I'd feel weird not being onstage with the rest of you."

"But it's *Lynne Vreeland*! It's your last chance to see her dance live," Leah cried, then instantly lowered her voice. The hall was still deserted, but the bare walls made everything echo loudly.

"Them's the breaks!" Kay said.

Leah was shocked to hear her sound so blasé. "But you can't just sit back and miss her. I mean, she's your—"

"Whatever she is," Kay broke in sharply, "I'll just have to miss her. Too bad, but well, that's my tough luck. I'll live."

Leah stared at the receiver. Had Kay Larkin, Lynne Vreeland's biggest fan, actually said that? A month ago Kay would have walked over burning coals to catch a glimpse of her heroine. Now she didn't even sound upset about missing the week of performances. And she didn't even want to come and watch from the best seats in the house.

"Leah, you still there?" Kay's voice sounded distant.

Leah pressed the receiver back against her ear. "Uh, yes. I'm here."

"So how'd it go today?"

"Okay," Leah answered quickly. "Kay, are you all right? I thought you'd be upset about this."

"I am upset, but there's nothing I can do about it. Listen, right now I'm just glad I didn't get hurt so badly I'll never dance again. A fall like this puts things in perspective."

A moment later Leah ended the conversation.

After hanging up she stood poised, one hand on the phone, trying to figure out what was wrong with her friend. Alex's suggestion that Kay had fallen on purpose suddenly began to seem right. Leah couldn't figure out why, but she was getting the distinct impression that Kay was almost happy to be missing Ballet Canada and the chance to meet Lynne Vreeland. She slowly made her way down the hall, not exactly sure where she was headed. As she sipped her diet soda, she mulled over Kay's behavior. Maybe Kay was just putting on a front, pretending everything was okay when inside she was really hurting. Leah couldn't blame her. If she were in Kay's position, she wouldn't want anyone feeling sorry for her either. Yes, Leah concluded, that was it. Kay was putting on a front, but maybe later, if she could corner Kay in her room alone, face-to-face, she'd encourage her to let her feelings out. It couldn't be good to keep her disappointment bottled up like that. Then Leah could tell her all about Lynne, and how kind she seemed to be. That might change Kay's mind, and get her to come to see at least one of her idol's performances.

Leah looked up and found herself outside the practice rooms. They were deserted, though all well lit. She peered up and down the concrete halls. She was alone. Breathing a sigh of relief, she pushed open the door to a small studio. She put down her soda and shoved her dance bag against the wall. She closed her eyes and tried to remember the steps to Princess Aurora's act one variation. Slowly, thoughtfully, she proceeded to the far corner of the room. Then, humming the music very softly, she began to dance. Halfway across the floor she stopped. After the arabesque, then what? Leah shook her head, and slowly sauntered back to her starting position. She stood lost in thought, her hands on her hips, trying to visualize the next combination of steps. She decided to try it from the beginning again. As she stepped into the opening arabesque, she heard a cough.

Leah gasped, and looked into the mirror, then behind her. "Oh! Miss Vreeland!" she cried, falling off pointe. Her hands flew up to her mouth.

"I'm sorry to disturb you," Lynne Vreeland said, smiling.

"Disturb me?" Leah gulped. "Oh, no. You didn't disturb me. I shouldn't be here." She made a move toward the corner and her dance bag.

"Why not?" Miss Vreeland put down her own bag. "The only way you become a really great dancer is to work at it every chance you get. *Every* chance," she emphasized. "But you look like you need a little help. Has Madame Preston taught you this variation yet?"

"No, we're learning the Rose Adagio but we haven't worked on the next part. I really haven't seen it since I was a kid, until today, that is."

"Let me show you." Miss Vreeland checked her delicate antique wristwatch, then began to mark the steps, naming them as she went.

Leah hung back only a second, but when Miss Vreeland looked at her in the mirror, she gained courage and walked through the variation, following the lead of the older dancer. She tried to match her movements to the prima ballerina's. She was surprised how natural the steps felt as she did them. Alex had always teased her that she was born to dance the role of Princess Aurora in

Sleeping Beauty. After all, a variation from the last act of the ballet had won her entrance into the Academy.

"Now you try. I'll count." In a soft musical voice the ballerina counted and sang the melody. "Very good." She clapped as Leah finished the first sequence of steps. "I think the role suits you. Someday that's what the critics will say." Miss Vreeland looked at Leah carefully. "How old are you?"

"Fifteen. I'll be sixteen in May," she added somewhat apologetically. She felt terribly young in front of Miss Vreeland, young and inexperienced and very far from being a great dancer. Monsieur Vuillard's favorite word, *provincial,* surfaced in her mind. How had Lynne Vreeland become so sophisticated, so worldly?

A hazy look clouded Miss Vreeland's large blue eyes. "At your age I dreamed of dancing so many ballets." She ambled over to the barre and stared into the mirror. With her pinky she erased a smudge of mascara from beneath her eye. "But the role I wanted to dance most when I was a very little girl was Princess Aurora," she continued in a dreamy voice. "I saw Fonteyn dance it one time in New York. I was so little I hadn't even graduated to my first pair of toe shoes. But that's when I knew I wanted to be a ballerina someday. It's funny to think I'm still dancing that role."

A note of sadness crept into Miss Vreeland's voice. Leah looked at her carefully. At the moment the great ballerina looked more like a slimmer, fit version of her own mother than a dancer portraying a sixteen-year-old. For the first time in her life Leah realized how awful it must be to someday be too old for dancing. Her instinct was to reach out and comfort Miss Vreeland, but Leah felt very young and awkward, and didn't know how. Being too old to dance was so foreign to her.

Lynne Vreeland stretched out the back of one leg, then suddenly straightened up. Briskly she massaged the nape of her neck and enveloped Leah in a smile. Her smile was warm and sincere and oddly familiar. "I bet you'll get to dance this role soon!"

Leah gaped at the dancer. "Me?" she gulped.

Miss Vreeland crossed the floor and rubbed some rosin on her hands, then ground the toe of each of her shoes in the flat wooden packing crate that served as the rosin box. "Yes, you," she stated firmly. "Madame Preston told me the school's spring gala performance will be *Sleeping Beauty*."

"Great!" Leah cheered aloud. She congratulated herself for being, for once, one up on Kay. Would she have news for the girls in the boardinghouse tonight!

"From what I've seen of your dancing, you won't have much competition for the role of Princess Aurora." Lynne looked at her critically and nodded her head before concluding, "Yes, you were really born for it."

Leah was speechless. Her head was swimming with the compliment. Lynne Vreeland had an awful lot of confidence in her. But why? Leah's skepticism must have shown on her face.

"You're the right body type, and you have such a pure classical line, like Fonteyn."

Leah shook her head in disbelief. "But I can't dance like that yet."

"Of course not," Miss Vreeland said matter-of-factly. "You're just a student. But I mean it. You've got the same sort of quality as Fonteyn and a lovely body. You'll go far."

Leah felt shy, embarrassed, and overwhelmed. She looked down at the floor, over toward the piano, then toward the door. She fought the impulse to run out and tell Katrina or Alex or Linda exactly what Lynne had just said to make it seem real and not like a dream. Leah took a couple of steps forward, her hand over her heart. It was pounding so hard she thought it would burst from her chest. "Uh, thank you," she said softly, so softly Miss Vreeland didn't hear her. The dark-haired woman was bent over her dance bag, pulling out one item after another: a hairbrush, a fluffy pink towel, makeup, a paperback copy of *War and Peace*. Leah gasped, wondering when such a busy ballerina found time to read such a long book.

Finally Miss Vreeland pulled out a plain black datebook. She looked inside, then checked her watch. She frowned. Almost on cue men's voices and heavy footsteps sounded in the hall.

Miss Vreeland's face relaxed. "There you are," she shouted, leaning into the corridor. A moment later a blond-haired dancer and a man carrying some music walked into the room.

Turning to Leah, Miss Vreeland said, "You'd better run along now. There's more rehearsing for you girls downstairs, and I've got some work to do," she added, motioning to the two men.

"This is Jules Crespin, my partner, and my accompanist, Harvey Rosensweig."

"Uh, hi," Leah said, stretching out her hand.

"And this"—Miss Vreeland gave Leah's sleeve a friendly tweak—"is my sweater."

"Oh! I forgot all about it!" Leah cried, and quickly peeled it off. She folded it neatly and handed it shyly to Miss Vreeland. The ballerina balled it up and tossed it on top of her bag. She approached the mirror and began fussing with her hair.

The accompanist was already at the piano playing some chords. Jules had gone to the barre and was warming up.

"Thank you again," Leah said, flashing a shy smile at Miss Vreeland's reflection.

She smiled, then turned around abruptly. "Leah, that is your name, isn't it?" Leah wondered how she knew, but nodded. "If you're not busy after the dress rehearsal tomorrow, and if you aren't too tired, why don't I take you out to lunch. It would be fun. I'd like to get to know you better."

Leah couldn't believe her ears. "Lunch, with you?" Leah knew she was grinning foolishly, but she didn't care. "Of course I'm not too busy, and I'm never tired. Well, hardly ever." She spoke so fast, the words tumbled out of her mouth. "I'd be honored," she concluded in an awed whisper.

"Good. Then it's a date!"

Leah hurried into the hall, not wanting to intrude on Miss Vreeland's practice time. Two doors down she stopped dead in her tracks. Miss Vreeland's cultured voice rang out down the corridor. "I tell you, Jules, that girl's a gem. She's not just a super dancer. She's the one young dancer

I've met in ages who isn't selfish. You should have seen her helping another girl in class today. To tell you the truth, I'm impressed. I really—" The slam of the studio door cut off whatever else Miss Vreeland was saying. But Leah had heard enough.

Her feet barely touched the floor as she sped down the hall. She raced up the back stairs two at a time. Andrew Maxwell's voice was ringing out over the loudspeaker. "Places, please. The prologue is about to begin."

Leah tossed down her bag and ran behind the backdrop to the opposite side of the stage. Wayne was waiting for her, one hand extended. With his other hand he was escorting Pam. Leah allowed herself to be led in a graceful promenade around the stage, but she was grateful when Wayne guided her back to their place in front of the towering throne-room columns painted on the backdrop.

All through rehearsal Leah couldn't suppress her smile. Her heart was singing. She glanced over at Pam. If Pam only knew! Lynne Vreeland had actually asked her to lunch. *And* she thought she showed promise. The Ballet Canada star had said she was a good dancer and had predicted that Leah would someday dance the role she had dreamed of dancing since she was a little girl in Hannah Greene's dance class. The idea that Lynne Vreeland had once shared the same dreams was almost overwhelming. *I can't wait to tell Alex,* she thought. And Kay. A momentary frown flitted across her face.

All at once she thought of just the thing to cheer her friend up. Tomorrow at lunch she'd tell Miss Vreeland about how her biggest fan at the school wouldn't be able to meet her because of a dumb injury. Maybe she could get an autograph for Kay. Leah giggled thinking of the surprised expression she'd find on Kay's face when she presented her with a personally signed photo of Miss Vreeland. Wayne tightened his grip on her hand and arched his eyebrows. Barely moving his lips, he asked, "What's up? Everything okay?"

"Oh, Wayne," she whispered a little too loudly. "I've never been better." Andrew cast a scathing glance in Leah's direction, but she was too excited to care and her smile grew even wider.

Chapter 8

Cocoa Nuts was jammed as usual on this Saturday night. Rock music blared from the vintage jukebox and Leah stood in the doorway of the popular SFBA hangout, hesitant. She wondered if she'd made a mistake coming here the night before dress rehearsal. Her costumes fit perfectly now, but if she broke down and indulged in one of Cocoa Nut's gooey desserts, Sylvie would have to work some last-minute magic on the seams. The tantalizing aroma of chocolate and other undefinable sweets wafted temptingly around her head. After a moment she spotted Alex's dark head, and next to her Katrina and Linda, wearing one of her funky broadbrimmed straw hats. Michael and Kenny were there and another boy Leah knew only by sight. Kenny was the first one to see her and he waved her over enthusiastically. Leah smiled and self-consciously put her hand to her hair. She wasn't sure she wanted anyone to notice what she had done to it. But if they didn't notice, she knew she'd feel let down.

"No luck with Kay?" Michael asked as Leah approached the round wooden table. Although the decor of the ice cream parlor suggested it was new, the surface of the table was carved with a generation's worth of kids' initials.

Leah traced an "LKS 71 luvs PJ 70" with her index finger and shook her head somberly. "She's holed up in her room. She wouldn't even let me in. I guess she's pretty depressed. I wish Melanie were around tonight. I hate to think of Kay all by herself moping over that injury, and in pain on top of it."

Kenny grabbed a chair from a nearby table and offered it to Leah. Leah settled herself between Katrina and Linda and waited for Alex to say something new about her hairstyle.

"I don't know why she's even bothering to mope," Alex said. Her full lips were turned down slightly, and she tapped a Cocoa Nuts matchbook impatiently on the table. "She got what she wanted, didn't she?"

"Alex, how can you say that?" Leah exclaimed, forgetting all about her hair.

"Well, you were there. I think she fell on purpose."

"Sorokin, you're nuts," Kenny remonstrated. He tilted his chair back and stared at Alex dubiously.

"Kay wouldn't purposely try to avoid Lynne Vreeland," Katrina said.

Alex threw her hands up in the air. "I didn't say she was trying to avoid Lynne Vreeland. I just think she's avoiding being around the company. But I don't know why." She tossed the matchbook back into the ashtray and slipped her hands into the pockets of her black jeans. She stared thoughtfully out the sweetshop's front window at the knots of passersby crowding the busy intersection. Suddenly she turned to Leah. "You know what I'm talking about. Kay's been acting weird ever since Madame's announcement about Academy students taking part in Ballet Canada productions. Everyone's noticed. What do you think is going on?"

Leah shifted uncomfortably in her chair. For some reason, she was hesitant to voice her own doubts aloud. She hadn't even told anyone about that afternoon's phone call to Kay. So all she said was, "I don't know. I think she's very upset. You know how excited she was a few days ago. Maybe she really worked herself up enough to get sick, and then to fall." Leah broke off, afraid to say more. She wanted to give Kay a chance to talk about her problems herself before she discussed them with anyone else.

"Speaking of sick," Linda suddenly interrupted. Holding the brim of her hat, she leaned forward and stared directly at Leah. "You look a little strange yourself. Are you feeling okay?"

"Who, me?"

"Leah doesn't look sick," Katrina said, peering intently at her from across the table. "You just look, uh, different," she added tactfully.

"Leah Stephenson!" Alex laughed heartily. "It's that awful eye makeup and your hair. What have you done to your hair?"

"Nothing," Leah said with dignity. "I just thought I'd try bangs. That's all."

Alex gave Leah a knowing look. "Bangs make you look like a little girl. The shape of your face is completely different from Ms. Vreeland's, you know."

"That's where I've seen that hairdo before," Katrina said, gasping. She reached up and patted the back of Leah's bun.

"I like it," Michael said loyally.

"As if you know the difference between one hairstyle and another, Litvak!" Alex scoffed.

"I just wanted to do something different."

"You could have died it black," Alex suggested evilly.

Linda picked up the joke and added with a wicked gleam in her eye, "And permed it. Curly dark hair, blue eyes. It might have had just the effect."

"Stop it," Leah said, growing peeved. She felt her face grow hot. Why did all her friends have to be mind readers? For one crazy moment in the drugstore this evening, she had almost bought a box of jet-black hair dye. The words "permanent hair color" in small type and the thought of her mother's reaction was all that stopped her. "Can't I try something new once in a while?" Catching the expression on Alex's face, she admitted with a sigh, "Okay, so I wanted to look like Lynne Vreeland. I think she looks wonderful. And my hair feels good this way. I don't think it looks *that* bad."

"Maybe not," Alex said archly. "But not that good either. And all that heavy makeup makes you look like the wicked fairy in the prologue to *Beauty*. Thick purple eyeshadow does not suit you. You're the natural, outdoorsy type."

"Outdoorsy type!" Leah wailed, and buried her head in her arms. "Spare me," she mumbled, face-down to the table.

Alex looked puzzled and checked with Linda.

"That is the right word, isn't it? Someone who looks like they don't wear makeup?"

Linda giggled and reassured Alex with a nod.

Leah raised her head, folded her arms across her chest, and decided to ignore Alex's comments.

After a moment's stony silence, Alex playfully jabbed one of Leah's new rhinestone stud earrings. "These are nice, though. Of course, *hers* are real diamonds."

"Someday mine will be real diamonds, too," Leah countered acidly.

Everyone at the table burst out laughing and Leah looked hurt.

Alex quickly softened her tone. "Come on, Leah, can't you take a joke. It's just that we're all used to Kay being the groupie around here. Not you. What's gotten into you?"

Before Leah could respond, Katrina said warmly, "Lynne Vreeland smiled at Leah in class because she danced so well today. If she had smiled at me like that, I'd do weird things to my hair, too." Katrina grimaced and rolled her eyes toward the ceiling. She clapped her hands over her mouth and said earnestly, "I didn't mean you look weird."

Leah gave a loud dramatic sniff. "How I look doesn't seem to matter to *some* people around here." She buffed her neatly trimmed nails on the sleeves of her patched denim jacket. She looked at each person around the table in turn. When she was sure she had gotten their undivided attention, she made her announcement. "Tomorrow yours truly is having lunch with—" She paused for dramatic effect. "—Lynne Vreeland!" Her haughty expression collapsed into a silly smile as everyone began talking at once.

"Huh?"

"How'd that happen?"

"You're kidding."

"Leah, how did you manage that?"

Leah propped her elbows on the table, and everyone leaned in to hear better. "I don't know how I managed it," she said honestly. "I really don't." Leah related the story of her two encounters with the star at the Opera House. "Then she asked me if I was busy after rehearsal. Can you imagine? The next thing I knew we were going to lunch. What do you think I should wear?"

"A skirt," Alex said instantly. "You don't know what kind of place she'll take you to."

Linda disagreed. "Leah looks best in pants. I love your new blue jumpsuit. Wear that. Believe me, she won't go anywhere too fancy in the middle of the day. She's got a lot of dancing to do and won't want to feel weighted from a lot of food."

"Did you tell Kay yet?" Michael asked.

Leah shook her head. "No. I didn't have a chance to. It's not the kind of thing you shout through a door at the boardinghouse."

Later that night, when all the girls were asleep, Leah crept barefoot down the creaky front stairs. After peeking into the darkened living room, and beyond, toward the equally dark alcove, a renovated sunporch that served as Pamela Hunter's bedroom, she tiptoed into the kitchen. She held the swinging doors so they made only the softest whoosh as they closed. Then she flicked on the tiny shaded lamp and laid her thin notebook with the black and white marbleized cover on the oilcloth-covered table.

She moved around the kitchen silently, first to the refrigerator to take out the milk, then over to Mrs. Hanson's spice rack. She poured a teaspoon of vanilla into a old chipped white enamel pan and measured out a cup of milk. She put it on the stove to heat, and, after a moment's deliberation, spooned in a generous serving of honey. Then she walked back to the table and sat down, drawing her feet up under her flowered flannel nightgown and thick terry robe.

She picked up her notebook and opened it. Her neat round handwriting filled more than half the pages. She pulled a ball-point out of her pocket and leaned forward on her elbows. Staring into space, she gnawed the end of the pen. So much had happened today. It was hard to organize her thoughts and write them down tonight. They were in such a wonderful jumble. She had tried unsuccessfully before climbing into bed, then when she couldn't sleep, she decided the less personal atmosphere of the boardinghouse kitchen might be better to write in. She didn't just want to record the events of the day, or her impressions about Lynne Vreeland. She wanted to think. Tomorrow she'd have the chance of a lifetime to talk one-on-one to a successful, internationally famous ballerina, someone whose dancing she really respected and who could shed a little light on what life was like outside the protective environment of a ballet academy, someone who could tell her what perils and pitfalls, as well as rewards, lay behind the gilded curtain.

Leah thought about her experiences since first coming to SFBA. She hadn't been here that long but already she felt completely different from the small-town girl who had first stood outside the elegant Victorian mansion that housed SFBA. She had had her first small but unnerving brushes with ruthless competition from other students, like Pam, vying for top positions in the class. And she had experienced firsthand with James the dire consequences of driving herself too hard trying to be the best. Until she had watched Lynne Vreeland in class this morning, she had almost forgotten what being a really great dancer meant: dancing under all kinds of circumstances, sometimes in grueling conditions, just for the joy of it. Although Lynne Vreeland would be retiring this season at the end of a long career, her dancing reflected pure happiness. Leah wanted to know how to become a professional dancer and still feel like that. Just below the surface she was seething with questions, but at the moment they stubbornly remained vague feelings that refused to be put into words.

She tapped her pen against the page, stared off into space, and tapped the pen again. A sizzling sound from the stove brought her to her feet. She dashed over and poured the hot milk into a mug. When she sat down again she picked up her pen and printed in big block letters in the top margin: TO BE A DANCER. Gripping her pen tightly and chewing her bottom lip, she began to scribble down the thoughts in her head.

A soft thud sounded on the stairs outside the kitchen. Leah sat up straight. She clutched her robe to her and stared at the kitchen door. A moment later it squeaked open. Looking pale, with dark circles under her blue eyes, Kay walked in. She spotted the light and stopped. She sagged slightly against the doorframe and rubbed her injured ankle with one hand.

"Uh, I didn't know anyone was here," she said, about to turn away.

"Kay, where are you going?" For a moment Leah simply stared at her. *The girl looks haunted!* Leah thought, startled. Then she jumped up. She took Kay's arm and led her to the chair. Kay leaned heavily on Leah and winced with each step she took. Leah pursed her lips. She and Alex had been wrong, she realized grimly. Kay wasn't faking this injury.

Kay settled down in the chair before saying anything. "I was hungry," she confessed simply. A ghost of her happy-go-lucky smile played around her pale lips.

"I'll make you something to eat." Before Kay could protest, Leah was at the refrigerator poking around for some leftovers. She smiled when she saw a container labeled KAY'S STASH—KEEP OUT—OR ELSE!!!. She opened it up and brought it to the table. "Do you want a sandwich?" She was glad Kay was eating, at least. It seemed like a good sign.

Kay bobbed her head. "I shouldn't have skipped dinner, I guess. I just didn't have the heart—"

Leah interrupted before Kay could go on. She refused to let Kay feel sorry for herself. It would just make her feel worse in the long run. "Of course you didn't," Leah soothed her friend. "It's hard having this run of rotten luck right now." As Leah talked, she spread mayonnaise on two thick slices of Mrs. Hanson's homemade bread and loaded on some deli meat from Kay's container. Out of the corner of her eye she watched her friend. She'd just been sick for a couple of days, what with her "flu" or whatever it was, and now this injury, but she looked like she had dropped at least five pounds. Leah stuffed in some more turkey slices, and handed the plate over to Kay.

Kay took a small bite and started to chew. Leah picked up her mug of warm milk and sat down beside her. She discreetly closed up her journal. It didn't seem appropriate to flaunt her bubbly jottings about Lynne Vreeland and her list of silly questions in front of Kay. She was obviously very depressed.

"Leah," Kay started after a strained silence. "I, uh—that is, what—"

"What is it, Kay?" Leah asked, making her friend face her. "You're upset about something. Is it just missing out on the performances?"

Kay shook her dark curls vigorously. She turned away from Leah and with one hand began twiddling a strand of hair. When she started to speak again, Leah knew she wasn't revealing what was really on her mind. Kay was avoiding her eyes, staring intently at her sandwich. With her index finger she jabbed the top slice of bread, poking holes in it. "I just feel so dumb. Getting hurt and all. What—what is everyone saying about me?" she asked in a small voice.

"Saying about you?" Leah repeated, stalling for time. She opted to tell Kay the truth, but just part of it. "Just that it's rotten luck, I guess."

"Is that all?" Kay asked.

Leah responded with a question of her own. "Is there something you want to talk about?"

Kay looked up sharply. "Why do you ask that?"

Leah rested her arms on her legs and leaned

closer to Kay. "Because we're friends. And you haven't been acting like yourself ever since I teased you about Lynne Vreeland the other day. Are you . . . are you angry with me?"

Kay's response was instant. "No, not at all."

A sigh of relief barely escaped Leah's lips before Kay took back her words. "Well, not really angry," she said slowly. She looked up at Leah through thick dark lashes. Her blue eyes were filled with sadness, pain, and anxiety. "Just hurt a little."

"I'm sorry, Kay. I didn't mean to hurt you." Leah felt terrible. Like everyone else around the school, Leah took Kay's good nature for granted. Her suspicions that Kay's sensitivities ran deeper than met the eye were proving true.

"I know that," Kay said sadly. "But I guess it makes it hard to face Lynne Vreeland." Kay sat up straight and looked Leah in the eye for the first time in two days. With great passion she declared, "I feel so foolish. I just keep thinking everyone must be pitying me, the Vreeland groupie missing out on a chance to meet her heroine. I haven't been happy about the idea of working with Ballet Canada. The thought of meeting someone so famous scares me. I guess I'm sorry I'll never know what Miss Vreeland is really like."

Leah debated with herself. Telling Kay about her lunch date with the star seemed wrong. Afterward, tomorrow night, maybe Kay's spirits would be higher and Leah could tell her about it then. But she could certainly describe how wonderful and generous Miss Vreeland was.

"She's great. I wanted to tell you all about it on the phone." Leah paused, but sensing Kay wanted her to continue, she went on. "I got to talk to her a little today. She's really great, very generous and kind. She even helped some of us learn steps." Leah edited her experience for Kay as she spoke.

"You're kidding?" Kay said, amazed. "I always thought older dancers were afraid of younger ones coming up behind them. I've read they're not very generous that way."

"Yeah, well, I think that's true sometimes." Leah's face grew thoughtful. One of the worst parts of her experience with James last month had been Diana Chen. The current rising star at the Bay Area Ballet was a teacher at the school. Diana, who had already had her sights set on James as her future partner, was threatened by Leah, and jealous of her, and as a result it hadn't been pleasant to work with her. Leah mentally compared Diana and Lynne Vreeland. "I think Miss Vreeland's probably beyond that. Maybe there's no point in her worrying anymore. She knows this is her last season. Maybe she never had to worry about real competition to begin with. I just don't know." After another pause, Leah added, "I only know I like her."

"I think I would like her, too," Kay said in a funny voice. "But I'm afraid to find out."

Leah was puzzled by Kay's words.

Kay went on to explain. "I'm afraid she won't live up to my expectations. I'd hate to have my idol turn up with clay feet, or"—Kay's giggle seemed forced—"concrete toe shoes."

Leah tried to accept Kay's explanation even though it didn't quite ring true. After a pause she stated with great certainty, "I think she'll live up to your dreams. I'm sure she will."

Kay pushed back her hair. "She couldn't possibly!" Kay said in a tone that left Leah mystified. "Listen, I feel pretty crummy. I'm taking a couple more aspirin and going to bed. Would you mind?" Kay pointed to the dirty plate and glass.

"Not at all. I'll wash them. You should stay off your feet." Leah waved Kay toward the door. Kay took a few steady steps, then started to limp again. The door swung closed behind her with a squeak and Leah held her breath waiting for Pam or Mrs. Hanson to appear. But no one stirred. Leah went to the sink with the dishes. She turned on the faucet and poured in some soap. As she began to scrub the enamel pan, the hall clock struck one. Leah tried to make sense out of Kay's explanation. She had admitted avoiding Miss Vreeland. But why? It couldn't have been just because the star might not live up to her expectations. Kay hadn't been lying about that, Leah could tell. But she hadn't been telling the whole truth either. And again Leah asked herself *why*. Why in the world would the chance to meet your favorite dancer cause such problems?

Chapter 9

Leah wasn't prepared for the crowd when she stepped out from the stage door the following afternoon. The wall of human bodies that blocked her way scared her. Lynne Vreeland groaned under her breath and maneuvered herself in front of the young dancer. The tired, peeved expression on Miss Vreeland's face vanished, and right in front of Leah's eyes she turned on the charm. Witnessing the transformation from a hardworking dancer to a beloved star with hundreds of fans made Leah vaguely uncomfortable, but she knew that being able to turn on charisma at will was a useful tactic. The effect of the ballerina's radiant smile was to make the sea of people part.

Lynne Vreeland's gracious skill in manipulating the aggressive group of fans impressed Leah.

"Would you lend me a pen. Oh, what a *dear* you are!" Miss Vreeland's voice rose ever so slightly. A balding young man handed over his pen and Lynne Vreeland favored him with a soft smile. You would have thought he had handed her a dozen roses rather than just a cheap ball-point pen, Leah observed. She stood right behind Miss Vreeland, shielding her eyes from the popping flash bulbs.

"Yes," Lynne Vreeland said to one fan. "I will be dancing two of the four *Swan Lake*s and three of the *Beauty*s." Inch by inch, while signing autographs, Lynne Vreeland managed to work her way toward the curb and a waiting cab.

"What's your name, dear?" Miss Vreeland met the small girl's saucerlike brown eyes and bent down. "Sarah? Is that with an *h* at the end?" Leah was almost as impressed as the child that a famous ballerina had cared enough to ask how she spelled her name.

"What are you doing here, Sam?" Lynne Vreeland stopped in her tracks and grabbed a man's hand. "Don't tell me you came all the way from Chicago?" Sam nodded happily. "I really appreciate that," the dancer said with genuine warmth. "Let's go for drinks after the matinee Wednesday. Pick me up at the stage door. I'll leave your name on the list."

Leah couldn't believe her ears. To think that people actually followed ballet companies from town to town. And the girls at SFBA called *Kay* a groupie! Leah was beginning to feel that the short but endless walk from the stage door to the curb was an education in itself. She was almost as impressed with Lynne Vreeland's ability to remember familiar faces and names as she was with the unflagging devotion of the fans.

"Can you hold this?" Miss Vreeland turned around and shoved her purse and a small carryall into Leah's hands. Leah smiled uncertainly. "I'll try," she said, wondering how to keep her own overladen dance bag up on her shoulder.

"Stay close," Miss Vreeland whispered out of the corner of her mouth. Leah tried not to let the fans come between her and the ballerina. The continual pressure of the crowd, the closeness of so many bodies pushing and shoving in such a small space made Leah a little dizzy. She blew a wips of blond hair off her face, wishing she had a free hand to wipe the beads of sweat off her forehead and upper lip. Leah had often imagined herself sweeping out of the stage door on the arm of a handsome partner, carrying roses and graciously signing autographs like this. The hectic scene was a far cry from her glamorous daydream. Just breathing was difficult. She forced herself to inhale deeply and pushed aside the fear that she might get crushed.

A light tap on her shoulder made her jump.

Leah turned her head quickly. A young woman with glasses poked a Ballet Canada yearbook under her nose. "Sign it," she commanded in a high voice. Her mouth formed a nervous smile. "Please," she added, putting a pen in Leah's already full hands.

Then another pen was shoved toward her, and another book. "Under your picture," one man begged.

Leah didn't know what to do. Her face reddened. "I can't ..." she started to explain.

"I'll hold your stuff," a boy offered. Leah tightened her grip on Miss Vreeland's purse and said a loud firm "No!"

Turning back to the girl with glasses, she smiled foolishly. "Thank you for asking for my autograph, but I'm not with the company. Really I'm not." A disappointed murmur rippled through the crowd. A second later all eyes were back on Lynne Vreeland.

After a few more difficult steps, Leah reached the curb. Her jumpsuit was clinging to her and little trails of sweat poured down her neck. The air was cool as usual but the press of the crowd around her made Leah feel warm. Lynne Vreeland opened the cab door and pushed Leah in. A second later she climbed in beside her and rolled down the window. Each gesture seemed so precise, so choreographed. Leah reflected that during her long career, Lynne Vreeland must have signed about a million autographs, and she had made an art of it. Miss Vreeland handed the autograph books back to the fans, then quickly rolled up the window. She tapped the cab driver on the shoulder and told him their destination. Slowly he pulled away. Miss Vreeland turned around and waved at the crowd through the back window. As soon as the cab turned the corner, she collapsed on her seat and pulled a tissue out of her pocket. With eyes closed she dabbed at her makeup, adjusted her earrings, and let out a sigh.

She looked incredibly tired and a little deflated. Leah wondered if having lunch with the ballerina was such a good idea. After strenuous morning rehearsals, she still had an entire afternoon of dancing ahead of her. And opening night was tomorrow.

Just when the silence threatened to grow uncomfortable, Miss Vreeland reached over and patted Leah's hand. "So how did you like your first autograph session?"

Leah gave a nervous laugh. "It wasn't *my* autograph session."

Lynne Vreeland chuckled. "Well, maybe not, but I saw them push those books at you. How did it feel, having people think you might be famous? Did you enjoy it?" Lynne Vreeland's eyes were shrewd as she waited for Leah's response.

Leah felt at ease under her gaze. She hadn't liked the crowd pestering her for autographs. But it thrilled her to think that people had taken her for a professional dancer. She also remembered what Kay had said last night about established ballerinas not always being generous to younger dancers. "It was a bit weird, I guess," she said finally, twisting the blue leather straps of her dance bag around in her hand. "Why were they trying to get my autograph?" she asked. The experience at the stage door had been exciting, but it left Leah feeling battered, hot, and confused.

"Fans are always looking for new stars." Lynne Vreeland was still eyeing her intently, and she had the feeling she was somehow sizing her up, the way dancers in class sized each other up. But Miss Vreeland was a famous performer, and Leah was just a student. She looked out the window down the hilly streets. Yesterday the idea of going out with Lynne Vreeland had seemed so right, so exciting, like a dream come true, the kind of thing she'd write about in a ten-page letter to her best friend, Chrissy, back home. Now that it was actually happening, Leah felt awkward and naive. She wasn't sure how to behave, or what was expected of her. Suddenly she saw herself as she must appear to Miss Vreeland: young, gawky, a high school kid with no life experience and little sophistication. Self-consciously she smoothed the pant leg of her jump suit. She had emerged from the crush of people looking rather wrinkled. A shy glance at Miss Vreeland revealed the dancer looked tired but jubilant. Her clothes weren't rumpled one bit. Suddenly Leah had a disturbing thought. Why was Lynne Vreeland bothering to take her to lunch? If she were a friend, Leah would ask her outright. That was Leah's style, to be up front, honest, and to the point. But Lynne Vreeland was a star, a dance-world VIP, and Leah felt increasingly inhibited beside her.

"You'll get used to the fans," Miss Vreeland said, rummaging in her bag, and pulled out a tortoiseshell hairbrush. "Don't ever forget they're your audience. They're the people you dance for in the long run." With quick nervous fingers, she pulled the pins from her top knot and removed the elastic band. A mop of thick, unruly curls tumbled down to her shoulders. She tugged the brush through a couple of times and fluffed up her bangs, then craned her neck to see the effect in the rearview mirror. Leah noted that with her hair hanging down softly around her face, she looked younger, not much older than Leah herself, although Leah knew she had to be about the same age as her mother. Miss Vreeland finally fished a bright pink scarf out of her bag and tied it with artful carelessness in her hair. She checked the mirror again and Leah watched, fascinated. She was wearing some wild glittery shadow on her eyes, and Leah made a mental note to buy some the next time she went to Paint, the makeup shop around the corner from the school. Leah self-consciously patted her own hair. She had worn it just like Miss Vreeland again, and now she wished she hadn't. If Miss Vreeland noticed, Leah would die. Still, Leah would give anything to look like the older dancer. She envied her dramatic looks and loved her casual style, though Leah was well aware it wasn't quite as funky as it seemed. The dangly diamond earring she wore in one ear was the real thing, the silk blouse and tight leather pants looked like they were very expensive designer fashions.

With one more brisk shake of her curls, Miss Vreeland put away her brush and faced Leah, apparently refreshed. "Crowds really take a lot out of me," she confided. She addressed Leah as an equal. "They're quite awful until you get used to them. It would feel strange to me now to come out of a stage door and find no one there. Once upon a time I'd leave by the service entrance to avoid the fans." She moistened her lips and frowned slightly, the faint lines in her forehead deepening for a moment. "I'll miss them," she said softly, almost as if she didn't want Leah to hear.

Leah folded her hands in her lap and wondered what to say next. Talking one-on-one to a star wasn't easy. Imagining long and brilliant conversations was one thing. Finding yourself in a cab next to a perfect stranger you knew nothing about besides what you'd read in various dance magazines was quite another. A sudden attack of shyness overcame Leah.

Lynne Vreeland quickly came to her rescue. She pointed a well-manicured finger toward a complex of modern white buildings leading down to the bay. "Have you been down to the Embarcadero yet?" Before Leah could answer, Lynne

Vreeland asked, "Are you from the Bay area?" When Leah shook her head, Miss Vreeland grinned. "Here we are, about to have lunch and I don't know the first thing about you except your name and that you won the Golden Gate Scholarship. I also know that you are a very promising young dancer with a particularly lovely arabesque." She pulled a five-dollar bill out of her purse and paid the driver.

Leah reeled from the compliment. *A promising young dancer with a lovely arabesque!* She'd write that in her journal tonight, on the last page, where she had begun a list of good things teachers and friends had said about her dancing.

A few minutes later Leah found herself seated across a white marble-topped table from Lynne Vreeland. The dark-haired ballerina had ordered Perriers and salads for both of them. "Don't want to feel too full before an afternoon of work!" she had explained before the waiter had even presented the menu. Leah looked around the restaurant, enjoying the light, airy decor. Green ferns hung in profusion in front of the windows and from high redwood beams. Exotic tropical birds squawked in elaborate wrought-iron cages overhead, and soft strains of chamber music wafted from loudspeakers tucked discreetly in the alcoved walls. She memorized the details to tell the other girls. She also wanted to put off any conversation. She was afraid she'd have nothing very important to say to such a famous person.

Slinging one arm around the back of her white wicker chair, Lynne Vreeland regarded Leah for a moment, then commented softly. "It's easier to talk in the studio than here, isn't it?"

Leah was momentarily taken back. Could the ballerina read her thoughts, or was she *that* obvious?

Miss Vreeland went on with a smile. "I always find it that way with other dancers." She propped her elbows on the table and cradled the frosty glass of mineral water between her hands. "In class the division between the stars and the members of the corps and other professionals just doesn't exist. You all work hard, you understand one another's problems, you help one another."

Leah colored slightly, remembering the compliment she overheard the other day in the hall. But Miss Vreeland's chatter was slowly putting her at ease. Leah cleared her throat and picked up the conversation. "I—I guess I keep wondering why you asked me here." Very quickly she added, "I'm really happy, I'm thrilled to be having lunch with you, but why me? You have so many other people to see and—"

The intensity of Lynne Vreeland's gaze cut Leah off. With a deliberate gesture she put her glass down. "Because I want to get to know girls your age, dancers your age. It's time I began to pass things on. To put it bluntly, I have connections, Leah, and I like what I've seen about you and your dancing. Maybe I can be of help someday." Leah's eyes grew large.

"I never even thought of that!" she blurted out.

Lynne Vreeland nodded at her approvingly. "I know. You aren't the conniving sort. I saw that right away. I'd like to think—" She broke off and fussed with her napkin, then with her hair. Finally she continued her sentence. "A daughter of mine might be something like you." There was a curious tenseness in her voice that belied her easy posture, the careless bohemian image she affected.

"That would be a lucky daughter!" Leah said passionately. "Having a dancer like you for a mother."

A dark look flickered across the ballerina's fair-skinned face. "Speaking of mothers, what does yours do, and your father?"

Leah looked down at her plate. Years had passed since her father's death, but it was still hard talking about him, especially to strangers. "My father died when I was little," she said, keeping her eyes down. After a quick intake of breath she was able to smile again. "My mother, well, she's just great!" Leah said with feeling. "We're pretty close. She runs her own computer consulting company back home. That's in San Lorenzo," Leah added, seeing the question in Miss Vreeland's eyes. "It's a farming community a couple of hours south of here. We're world famous for—" Leah put her hand to her mouth and tried to stifle a giggle. "You'll never believe this—*artichokes!*"

"I just love artichokes," Miss Vreeland responded with a hearty laugh. "Now I'll think of you every time I eat one," The waiter brought the salads, and Miss Vreeland squeezed some lemon on top of hers. Leah eyed the blue cheese dressing, but pushed it aside with a sigh and followed Miss Vreeland's example. Leah didn't have to worry much about her weight, but she was determined to learn all she could from the older dancer. She would force herself to like lemon on lettuce if it would help her look like Lynne Vreeland.

"And you first studied ballet in San Lorenzo?"

Leah nodded, her mouth full of spinach, and proceeded to tell Miss Vreeland about Hannah Greene's School of Dance and Theatre Arts, and her best friend, Chrissy, and getting accepted into the San Francisco Ballet Academy this past September. By the end of her story she was feeling perfectly at home with Miss Vreeland. The older dancer really did seem interested in the details of Leah's life. Leah found herself talking easily about her problems so far at the school: her run-ins with Pam, Diana Chen, and James. But she was careful not to mention any names.

When she had finished her salad, Miss Vreeland ordered coffee for herself and fruit for Leah and leaned back in her chair. She propped one foot up on a neighboring seat, and said with great charm, "But I've been asking all the questions. Tell me, is there anything I can do to help you? The Joffrey's in town. Are you auditioning? Do you want me to put in a good word? The director and I are friends."

Leah instantly shook her head. "No. I mean . . ." Her voice trailed off. She looked down at her plate. She wondered how Pam, or even Alex, would react if Lynne Vreeland had asked them that. But to her the answer was perfectly clear. "I'm just a student, Miss Vreeland. It's too soon for me to audition for a company. I have so much to learn. I'm not ready yet."

Lynne Vreeland arched her finely penciled brows and said quietly, "You are an intelligent girl, Leah. Taking advantage of more training with Madame is probably the best thing you can do. But the offer will still hold two or three years from now, when you will be more than ready to launch a career."

"I'll remember that," Leah said earnestly, her heart pounding at the prospect of launching a career at the time most kids would just be graduating from high school. "And thank you. But there is one thing—" Leah hesitated.

"Go on," Miss Vreeland urged.

"Well, it's something my mother said, and something I've been thinking about ever since I got here." Leah paused to choose her words carefully. She might never get the chance to ask a ballerina this kind of question again. "People keep telling me how much I'm giving up by choosing to be a dancer. At first I didn't think much of it, but sometimes I wonder if my mother was right." Leah tried to sort out her thoughts. What appealed to her most about Miss Vreeland was the sense that she had much more to her than her dancing. Was that just an accident? How did it happen? How did she find time to grow into the complicated person she seemed to be? "I feel," Leah said tentatively, "my life's a little limited at SFBA. It's narrower somehow than at San Lorenzo High. There's so much I don't know about: life, people, what makes the world tick. Sometimes I hear about countries on the news and I don't even know where they are," Leah confessed in an embarrassed voice. "Romeo and Juliet lived in Verona, and I had to ask my friend, Alex, what country that was in. I feel so stupid." The look of understanding on Lynne Vreeland's face made it easier for Leah to continue. "I just don't seem to have enough time to learn everything. I can barely keep up with my homework here. And then, what about people? Everyone I know is a dancer. I don't have time for anyone else. How can I ever dance the part of someone in love, for instance, if I never even have the chance to go out on a date? Even if I wanted to meet boys here at the school, there are so few—"

"I've noticed!" Miss Vreeland said, and suddenly Leah didn't feel quite as dumb revealing her fears about her career.

"And I never even get the chance to meet other kids. There's no time, and even if there were a little, say on weekends, I'm so tired by Saturday night. My whole life at SFBA is dance. I love it, though, and I wouldn't change a thing. But sometimes, when I'm having trouble in class, or when things are going badly, I wonder if it's worth it." Leah leaned forward in her seat and folded her hands on the table. Her blue eyes searched Miss Vreeland's intensely.

Miss Vreeland dropped her gaze and bit her lip. Suddenly she looked as uncertain and confused as a ten-year-old. "That's a tough question," she said after a moment's silence. "To tell you the truth," she went on, looking over Leah's shoulder and staring into space, "I don't really know the answer."

"But you've had a wonderful career, you've had everything!" Leah cried, astonished. "You must know!"

Lynne Vreeland shook her head, then took a deep breath. "Well, I can tell you two things. I've made some mistakes—some big mistakes—in my personal life. I was younger then and might do things differently now. I don't know. But even so, I would say it has been worth it for me."

Leah breathed a sigh of relief. Then Miss

Vreeland went on. "But that's my life, Leah. Only *you* know what's right for you. Unfortunately, there are no guarantees in the dance world. You have to make some pretty big decisions when you're far too young to know what you are giving up. And things do happen—accidents, injuries. You have to somehow be prepared for that. Make up your mind not to look back, no matter what happens, and no matter what choices you make." Miss Vreeland's voice sank to a whisper. For a moment Leah thought she was going to cry. But the moment passed, and when Miss Vreeland met her eyes again, she looked every inch the warm, charming, self-assured star.

"So then, it is worth it, no matter what." Leah had to make sure she had gotten it right. She had to know.

Lynne beamed at her. "Yes, no matter what. And that's exactly what I would tell my own daughter."

Chapter 10

Later that evening Leah sat cross-legged on the floor in the boardinghouse parlor telling her friends about her lunch with Lynne Vreeland. "I feel like a girl in a fairy tale." She stopped to blow on a steamy spoonful of soup, then put the spoon back into her bowl without taking a mouthful. How could she possibly eat feeling like this, as if she were floating a good two feet off the ground. "You know the one where an enormous fish rises out of the sea and grants three wishes?"

"What'd you wish for? And who may I ask is the big fish?" Kay hobbled in with her tray. Sunday night was always potluck at Mrs. Hanson's. Dinner was informal. The girls invariably gravitated toward the living room with dinner trays and ate with the TV on. Tonight, however, the star attraction wasn't on the screen.

From her chair in the corner, Pam emitted a loud groan. "Haven't you heard the news, Larkin? Once upon a time a girl couldn't sneeze in this place without you being the first to hear."

Kay didn't spare Pam a look. She gratefully accepted the chair Melanie vacated, and propped her foot up on a plump leather hassock. Then she reached for her salad and speared a chunk of hard-boiled egg. "So aren't you going to tell me?" Kay addressed Leah, then bit heartily into her egg. "You look like you're in love or something!" Kay mumbled, reaching for her juice.

Leah couldn't hold back a smile.

"Wrong, Larkin!" Alexandra chuckled. "But I'm not going to be the one to break the big news."

Before Leah could speak for herself, Pam let out a very loud sigh. "Well, I will. Have some sympathy. The girl's been sick. We don't want her to die of suspense, do we? Leah has stolen your thunder, Kay." Pam pretended to think. "No, perhaps stepped into your role is more like it," she said with a self-satisfied smirk, standing up to stretch her muscular body before dropping down again onto the sofa. "Leah finagled lunch today with the great, illustrious, most famous has-been in balletdom, Miss Lynne Vreeland!"

"Oh, shut up!" Melanie glared at Pam.

Pam wasn't fazed. She balled a pillow under her head and rolled over onto her side. Her sharp eyes watched for Kay's reaction.

"You what?" Kay's soft-spoken response took everyone by surprise.

"I did, Kay. I would have told you last night, but—" For the life of her, Leah couldn't figure out why she sounded so apologetic. But the look on Kay's face scared her. "I wanted to surprise you. I got you this." She reached down into her bag and produced a glossy publicity shot of the famous dancer. The ballerina's handwriting was big and bold and sloppy, but very legible: TO KAY, A PROMISING DANCER IN HER OWN RIGHT, HOPE YOU FEEL BETTER SOON, L. VREELAND.

Kay sat up straight and gaped at the picture, then looked at Leah.

"How nice!" she said, not sounding at all as though she meant it.

Leah's heart sank. "I—I thought you'd like it."

"It was very thoughtful of you," Kay said stiffly, and poked around in her salad. Apparently nothing in the dish seemed to interest her and she put the plate down on the table. The clatter rang out in the silent room.

"At least someone around here has come to their senses about that dancer," said Pam. "She should have quit years ago. That's what my teacher back home always said. It's better to stop while people remember you at your best."

"Good advice," Alex interjected in a cold tone, "and from what I saw, Miss Vreeland is still at her best. I'm sure if she had asked you to lunch, you might have something quite different to say."

Pam sat up and glared at Alex. Before she could speak, Melanie made an impatient gesture with her hand. "Would you girls stop it? Give Leah a chance to tell us what she's like. Did she let her guard down? What did you talk about? I'd be tongue-tied around someone so famous." Melanie smiled encouragingly at Leah.

After a puzzled glance at Kay, Leah began. "I felt just like that, Melanie. I was scared to death I wouldn't know what to talk about. But she made me feel relaxed. As if it didn't matter I was just a kid and she was a star. We talked about lots of things." Leah didn't mean to be evasive, but she

felt the important parts of her talk with the ballerina had been private—about offering her help
someday, about her own potential as a dancer,
about learning that all the difficulties that lay
ahead were really worth it. "She seemed really
interested in my home, where I came from." Leah
giggled. "I couldn't believe it, she even seemed
interested in San Lorenzo's artichoke farms."

"Spare me!" Pam rolled her eyes and got up
from the sofa.

All the other girls except Kay started laughing.
"That's one woman who looks like she's never
been within ten miles of a farm. Did she tell you
about herself?"

Alex's question stopped Leah dead. "No," she
said after a moment's reflection. "Not really. A
little about her dancing. How she'd miss her fans."
Leah paused and grew thoughtful. Then she continued dreamily. "She made me feel that becoming a great ballerina was worth whatever it takes."

"She said that?" Kay asked in a shrill voice.

Everyone looked at her in surprise. Kay was
standing up, facing Leah, her face livid.

"What's the matter, Kay?" Leah asked, slowly
rising to her feet.

"The matter?" Kay laughed with unaccustomed
bitterness. "I'll tell you what's the matter. The
woman's not worth this fuss you're making over
her. I know more about her life than you do—"
Kay stopped short, then started again, her blue
eyes dark with anger. "She's a liar. A career like
hers is *not* worth it, and she above all people
should know that!"

Kay stomped from the room and raced up the
stairs, taking them two at a time.

Pam voiced what everyone was thinking. "What happened to her sprained ankle?"

Alex jumped up to follow Kay, but Leah put out a hand and stopped her. "No," she said in a low, firm voice, "let me. She'll talk to me. I'm sure of it."

Leah left the room not feeling sure at all, but she was determined to get to the bottom of Kay's problem, whatever it was. Last night Kay had been on the verge of confiding in her. She had suspected Kay was pretty upset about something, but she hadn't thought it would be this serious. She paused at the foot of the stairs for a moment, then heard Pam's silky drawl from behind her as she started for the second floor. "If you ask me, dear sweet Kay is downright jealous. She'd cut off her right arm to spend ten minutes alone with Lynne Vreeland, and then Leah goes and gets asked to lunch." Pam's laugh disgusted Leah, and she quickened her pace up the steps.

"Kay, let me in," Leah pleaded through the closed door. She could hear Kay inside, crying. She also heard drawers opening and slamming shut. "Kay!" she raised her voice a little. When she still didn't respond, Leah resorted to threats. "If you don't let me in, I'm getting Mrs. Hanson. I'm—we're all worried about you. I'm not going to let you go to sleep like this. Besides, Melanie has to get in later. You can't lock her out all night!"

The key turned in the lock. Leah waited a moment, then pushed the door open and went in. Kay was standing with her back toward her, at the balcony. The French doors were open and a chill but refreshing breeze blew in from the bay. The Golden Gate Bridge twinkled in the night. As

Leah waited for Kay to acknowledge her presence, she watched the distant reflection of lights dance on the dark water.

"Kay, please talk to me," Leah began gently. She walked over to Kay's rocking chair and tossed off the pile of tights and clothes. She sat down quietly, then caught her breath. Kay's three unwieldy duffel bags were open at the foot of her bed. "Are you going somewhere?" Leah asked, afraid to hear her answer.

Kay didn't reply. She stood at the window, so still she looked like a statue.

Leah searched her mind for something to say, some way to reach this new silent Kay.

"I know you're upset about my going to lunch with Miss Vreeland—" Leah began.

"*You* have nothing to do with it," Kay said with force. She wheeled around and faced Leah. Her face was contorted into a hurt, pained expression. Leah wanted to rush up to her, hug her, but something about Kay said hands off.

Making no effort to hide the fact she wasn't limping, Kay walked over to the bed. Without looking at Leah she began folding her underwear and placing it in neat little stacks. She picked up a suitcase and with sharp deliberate movements began to pack. Leah stood up and began to help her. If Kay wanted to leave, Leah wanted to know why, but she wouldn't try to stop her.

With Leah by her side she began to talk. "I'm sorry I've been taking this all out on you." Her voice was tight and thin and matched her movements. "I'm not upset about you. I'm upset with—with Miss Vreeland." The name sounded strange and twisted on Kay's lips. Leah stopped midway in rolling up a pair of tights. She stood very still, sensing Kay was finally about to break down, to tell her at least what was going on.

"You see, Leah." Kay looked up and faced Leah, her eyes bright with tears. "Miss Vreeland might think a dance career is worth it, worth all the pain and trouble you cause other people, but to me, nothing, nothing in the world excuses what she did."

"What she did?" Leah repeated confused.

"She left my father. She left me." Kay's voice strained to finish the sentence. "Lynne Vreeland is my natural mother."

Leah sank down on the bed, not taking her eyes off of Kay. "You can't—" She was about to say Kay couldn't mean that. It was some sort of crazy story, like a lie someone might invent to create a romantic past. But Leah knew Kay was telling the truth. The resemblance hadn't been in her imagination—the deep blue eyes, the dark curly hair, the light dusting of freckles on her nose.

"Your mother!" she cried as the truth sank in. Leah jumped up and gave an involuntary shiver. Why hadn't Kay ever told her before?

Miss Vreeland had said something about the advice she would give her own daughter, but Kay was her daughter. And she hadn't mentioned the existence of Kay at all. "I don't get it!" Leah said, her voice shaking. She sat down again heavily and wrapped her arms around herself. "Kay, why haven't you mentioned this until now?" Suddenly Kay's behavior over the past few weeks began to make sense and a new thought formed in Leah's mind. "When did you find out about this?"

Kay didn't answer. She turned her back on Leah and began emptying her desk drawer.

"How long have you known?" Leah suddenly had to know all the details. The idea that Kay was Lynne Vreeland's daughter and had kept it a secret scared her.

Kay shrugged. Her voice was muffled as she answered. "I've always known. My father didn't keep it from me."

"But then why didn't she come and see you, be with you. I—I don't understand."

"She wanted to." Kay turned around. Tears brimmed out of her eyes, but she looked so hurt, so tragic, Leah knew no hug could take away the pain she felt.

Kay rubbed her sleeve across her nose and swallowed hard. "I didn't want to see her. When I was old enough to know about her, to know my mom wasn't my real mother, I was old enough to be angry, I guess. I think I hated her. How could someone leave a baby, a year-old baby, and a man as wonderful as my dad? I couldn't understand that. I still can't." Kay paused and reached for some tissues. She blew her nose hard. When she was finished, the silence in the room was broken only by the ticking of her bedside clock.

"She wrote to me. I still have the letters. But I've never shown them to anyone, not even my dad. She wanted to get to know me." Kay lowered her voice to a whisper. "I never answered them. I didn't want to have anything to do with her. One time she wrote my father and invited us to a performance in Philadelphia. It was that big gala when Alex's parents made their first appearance in the United States after their defection. I wouldn't go." Kay wound a tissue around her fingers. When she looked up at Leah, a smile crossed her lips. "I might have met Alex back then, when I was ten."

Leah tried to smile back, but her mouth felt tight. A hard angry knot was forming inside of her, right in the middle of her chest. She felt like she wanted to scream. How could Lynne Vreeland have done this to Kay, wonderful, lovable Kay?

"So you never saw her dance in person," Leah said, suddenly understanding why the Ballet Canada season had been so important to Kay until she found out that she was supposed to be onstage with Lynne Vreeland. "Oh, Kay, this all must have been so awful for you," Leah cried.

"Yeah. You can't imagine how much time I've spent wondering what I did to have my mother walk out on me like that. But that's what she did. My father told me it was her decision to leave. She felt she couldn't have both a family and a career."

Leah recoiled from Kay's statement. It was what she had always feared. She had never thought about having kids. That seemed too far away, but love? How could there be time for a relationship? She had asked herself that. She had asked Lynne Vreeland this afternoon. Now that she thought of it, had Miss Vreeland really answered that question? Suddenly Leah couldn't remember.

Kay went on in a soft voice. "Of course, I've never known any mom but the one I have. I never thought of her as a stepmother. My brothers and sisters, they're real family. I—I guess this all shouldn't bother me so much," she said. "I mean, I do have a wonderful family." She looked up at Leah. "But at the same time, I've always wanted to know everything about her—because, as you said, I look like her. And I'm a dancer, too. It makes me feel a little crazy, wanting to know all about her and not wanting to know her at all." She combed her fingers through her thick curly hair and once again met Leah's eyes. "I just couldn't stand it downstairs right now, when you started talking about how great she is. I realized how much I hate her. I didn't want you to like her at all."

"I guess I don't now," Leah said bitterly. "I mean, you're right. She is a liar. I feel like telling her that myself."

"No!" Kay shouted and grabbed Leah's arm. "Promise me you won't tell a soul about this. I couldn't bear for the other kids like Pam Bigmouth to know. I just want to leave here and let people make up their own reasons about why I split."

Kay's eyes were begging Leah to agree, to keep her mouth shut. A warning bell went off in Leah's head. James had begged her not to tell anyone about his problem, his injury, and look what had happened. They both got in trouble. Some instinct told Leah that Kay needed help, and yet, how could she betray this confidence? With great reluctance she finally said, "Okay, I promise. I won't tell anyone, Kay. But I don't see why you have to leave. No one knows about Lynne and you. You can just keep avoiding her. It's only for a week. Get sick again—"

Kay quickly looked away, an embarrassed flush stealing up her neck and face.

"Oh, Kay," Leah confessed, "Alex and I figured it out—about faking a fever with the thermometer and all. But we'll cover for you." Leah had no idea what she'd tell Alex, but she'd figure out something by morning. "Leaving here won't solve anything."

"You don't understand, do you?" Kay mumbled. "I don't want to be a dancer anymore. Thinking about it these past few days, what it means, what I'll be giving up, and the possibility of hurting people the same way she hurt me—well, I don't want to do that. And Leah, in my book," Kay said, a determined look in her eyes, "the chance of being a star isn't worth it."

Leah pondered Kay's predicament. Leaving SFBA would be all wrong for Kay. She hadn't only inherited her mother's looks, she had inherited a great deal of her talent, along with her own distinctively beautiful style of movement, her great speed, and swift feet. Kay was a promising dancer, no doubt about it. And if she would only be more serious, work harder. Suddenly Leah understood. "Kay," she said tentatively. "You haven't been sure of your career all along, have you?"

"No," Kay admitted.

"That's why you goof off so much." She rumpled Kay's hair and took a deep breath. "I think you've got some pretty intense stuff to deal with. Hearing about Lynne leaving you like that makes me angry, too. But you can't let your anger get in the way of everything else in your life. That was fifteen years ago. She hasn't got anything to do with you anymore. Not really." With each word she spoke, Leah grew more and more certain she was on the right track. "It's a little strange that you followed her career so closely and have the scrapbook and—"

"I know that. I couldn't help it," Kay interrupted, slamming her fist down on the bed. "I wanted to know what she was like. Part of her is inside me. Maybe that's why I dance." She lowered her voice again. "Maybe that's why I have to stop dancing." She sounded so morose, Leah felt certain for Kay not to dance was absolutely wrong.

She racked her brains a moment, then hazarded a small smile. "Kay, I tell you what. I promise not to tell anyone about this, not Alex, not Melanie, not Mrs. Hanson, not anyone. But you have to promise me one thing. Don't leave SFBA." Kay started to protest, but Leah put a finger to Kay's lips. "Hear me out. Don't leave yet. Wait a little while. Let all this commotion die down. Ballet Canada will be gone soon, then maybe we can talk about this again. Maybe—" Leah hesitated. "Maybe you should talk to someone about it. If not Madame, then Mrs. Hanson."

"Never!" Kay was adamant.

Leah sensed it was better not to argue with Kay just then. "Okay. But promise me you won't leave here yet. I won't tell anyone your secret if you promise me that."

Kay got up and rubbed her palms against her pants, then went over to the balcony doors. She put one hand on each of the intricately patterned knobs and stared out into the bay. The fog was rolling in but the bridge lights were still faintly visible. Her back heaved as she sighed. Then she shut the doors and turned around. "I promise," she said, then added in a small fearful voice, "do you?"

With deft, deliberate movements, Leah tore out four pages of her journal. Outside a church bell chimed twelve times. It was midnight, the start of a new day, a day on which Leah vowed never to mention Lynne Vreeland's name again. She tore the offending journal pages—the ones where she gushed on about the star—into tiny pieces, then tossed them into her wastepaper basket. The bits of paper fluttered slowly down like snow, landing on top of a pair of hopelessly torn tights and last night's first attempt at conjugating her French verbs.

The gesture was calculated to make her feel better. It did for a moment, then the numbness set in again. Leah couldn't get her mind off Kay, looking so small and defeated and heartbroken as she sat downstairs on the edge of her bed. She wondered if the tale she and Kay had concocted to tell the other girls sounded too made up. It was going to be especially hard to convince Melanie, Kay's warm, supportive roommate, that Kay's trauma over Ballet Canada and her outburst about Vreeland had to do with a boy in the corps named Wayne.

But as sorry as Leah felt for Kay, she felt angrier with herself. She had fallen hook, line, and sinker for Lynne Vreeland's glamorous image. She had seen her as the beautiful, poised prima ballerina dispensing advice at the end of a career as if she were talking to her own daughter. Leah shuddered to think that she had actually used those words. Would she have actually had the nerve to tell Kay Larkin to her face that being a dancer was worth it? Leah shook her head. Why had she ever gotten married in the first place?

Leah flicked out the light and flopped facedown on her bed. Her mother had sent her an old thick quilt in the mail and it had arrived earlier that day. It still smelled faintly of home. The familiar clean scent made Leah want to cry. Why was everything in the world of dance so complicated? Why weren't people ever what they seemed? Until she got to SFBA, Leah had thought the will to dance had been a sacred thing, to treasure. Now she was beginning to wonder if it was some kind of curse.

She sat up and hugged the bulky blue and purple comforter to her chest, then stared out her window into the swirling wall of fog, lost in thought. She remembered a famous ballet movie, *The Red Shoes*, that was about a curse. The ballerina ended up dancing her way to her own death, powerless to stop it. A strangled sob escaped from Leah's throat. She threw herself down on her stomach and wept long and hard into her pillows. She had always thought to dance, especially to dance her best, was to be happy. But it seemed the life she had to lead to dance would make her a sad person, and possibly not a very nice one. Lynne Vreeland radiated so much warmth and truth and love on the stage, but off stage she must not be a very nice person. She must have hurt Kay's father very badly, almost as much as she had hurt Kay.

The thought of Kay made Leah dry her eyes. She blew her nose and sat cross-legged on her bed, wrapping her quilt around her shoulders. Kay had forced her to promise not to tell anyone about her problem. Still, she couldn't forget how things had gone with James. He had needed help, but he, too, had made Leah promise not to tell anyone about his problem. But the help Kay needed was different. What if Leah's decision to abide by her promise hurt her more in the end?

Leah crawled between the sheets, but sleep was a long time coming. She kept thinking of the heroine in *The Red Shoes,* and as she drifted off into dreams, the star of the movie looked sometimes like Kay, with wild, dark hair, and sometimes blond and long-limbed like herself, as she danced to her terrible fate in her red satin shoes.

Chapter 11

Pamela must have been right, Leah thought the next morning as she trudged up and down the hilly streets leading from Mrs. Hanson's to the War Memorial Opera House. Her face wore a hard, angry expression and her knees hurt. The day she and Pamela had first arrived in San Francisco, Pamela had told Leah that walking was bad for a dancer's knees. Leah had scoffed at such a notion. But now it seemed Pam may have been right. Before coming to SFBA and taking two, sometimes three dance classes every day, six days a week, Leah's knees had never hurt. Somehow the thought that getting better as a dancer meant getting worse at a normal human activity—like walking—irked Leah. When she had decided she was going to become a ballerina, Leah hadn't known what she was giving up. Her mother had warned her, had told her all about growing up too soon, missing out on a normal teenage life just for the slim chance that a dream of dancing professionally might come true. But then, she couldn't forget that the wonderful Lynne Vreeland had said dancing was worth anything. Well, that was a joke. Leah let out a tight, sarcastic laugh that was instantly swallowed up by the wind.

She rounded the corner onto Van Ness and tightened her grip on her dance bag. With her other hand she turned up the collar of her slicker and pulled down the broad brim of her hat. Beneath her hat Leah's hair was up in its usual high topknot and her eyes were free of makeup. She had tried to pin her new bangs back out of sight. It would take a year to grow them out, she thought, disgusted. She hated herself for ever trying to look like Lynne Vreeland. Angry tears streaked down her face as she walked through the icy drizzle that sometimes fell as rain, sometimes hung still in the air as dense fog. In spite of the awful weather, Leah had chosen to walk the two miles rather than take the bus for a couple of very good reasons: one, walking was the best way she knew to work off her anger; and two, choosing to attend company class at the Opera House before today's dress rehearsal meant skipping Madame's class at school. She knew Lynne Vreeland would be there and she would do anything to avoid seeing her.

Unfortunately, the walk did little to clear Leah's head. She was angrier than ever when she got to the Opera House but at least she knew she wouldn't have to worry about seeing Lynne anytime soon. Dress rehearsal was scheduled half an hour after class ended. The company's gala opening was this evening. Leah didn't know how she'd manage to avoid Lynne then, but she'd figure out a way. Leah Stephenson never wanted to talk to Lynne Vreeland again.

*   *   *

Leah sat limply on the long wooden bench that ran the length of the corps members' dressing room. Sylvie stood behind her, considering the effect of Leah's wig in the mirror. "Now, look, *chérie,*" she said patting the tall white powdered mound of curls. "Eeeze theeze not *magnifique?*"

Reluctantly Leah met her own glum reflection in the mirror. Towering eighteenth-century-style wigs and a whole drawerful of stage makeup couldn't bring the sparkle back to her eyes or a smile to her face. Her lips were turned down in a thin, tight frown. As Sylvie fussed with the profusion of synthetic curls, Leah sat with her arms folded across her chest. "What eeze wrong? You don't like the look?"

"I don't feel very well today," she lied.

"Wait until tonight, when the lights go down in the house and you hear the overture on the other side of the curtain. You'll feel better then. I am sure of it." Sylvie powdered Leah's nose and helped her to her feet. "Now, you go to the rack and get your dress. Joelle, she will help you dress, *non?* And don't you worry, *ma petite,* it eeze just stage fright."

When Leah got to her feet it felt as if someone else were walking inside her body. Her struggle not to yell and scream and shout and tell the world that Lynne Vreeland was a fraud was wearing her out. She felt as if she had taken six of Madame's classes in a row. With Joelle's help she stepped into her costume and allowed herself to be zipped up. As soon as she was dressed, she walked out of the overheated, overcrowded room into the damp hall. She walked a short distance and turned a corner, finding herself in a deserted cul-de-sac. Perfect. No one would find her here, and she was close enough to the stage to hear Andrew's call for the start of dress rehearsal.

Not caring if the dirty concrete left a mark on the fine brocade of her dress, she sank down to the floor and leaned her head back against the wall. The wig made her feel top-heavy and cumbersome. She closed her eyes and thought about Kay. Since last night a tight hard knot had formed inside Leah's chest. How could Lynne have done this to Kay? How could she have ruined lives for the sake of her own career? Her eyes pressed tightly shut, Leah let out a hollow laugh. How would Lynne Vreeland answer those questions? Would she still have the nerve to tell her it was all worth it?

The sound of footsteps in a nearby corridor roused Leah. She struggled to her feet and shook out her dress. She listened to the footsteps approach, then die down in the distance.

She pressed her hands to her eyes and let out a low moan. The most awful thing was that no matter what she had seen over the past couple of days, no matter what she had learned, dancing still meant more to her than anything. It was a terrible, frightening thought. Did loving to dance mean having to live her life as Lynne Vreeland had lived hers?

"Why, Leah, dear, where were you this morning?"

Leah dropped her hands from her face and found herself eye-to-eye with Lynne Vreeland. She straightened up and pushed herself away from the wall. The expression on her face was defiant. Abruptly she turned her back on the dancer and marched toward the short flight of steps leading to the stage with her head held high.

"Leah!" Leah took a deep breath and whirled around at the sound of Madame's voice. She hadn't noticed the teacher standing there beside Lynne. Could she disobey Madame? She knew she was taking a terrible risk, but she stood her ground and flounced on up the stairs without responding. With great satisfaction she reflected that today Lynne didn't look very glamorous at all. The lines around her eyes were more pronounced, and her heavy makeup made her look old and ugly.

Leah walked into the wings and breathed deeply, waiting for rehearsal to begin. She patiently counted the floorboards that ran the length of the stage. Counting things, flowers on wallpaper, fish on shower curtains, had always been Leah's way of calming down, of getting her mind to stop rehashing her problems over and over again. Today it wasn't working.

"Leah." Madame's voice intruded on her counting. She had followed Leah upstairs. Leah's heart seemed to stop but she forced herself to meet Madame Preston's gaze. Madame's angular face held no hint of kindness. She looked cold as a glacier and as dangerous. She hadn't looked like this even when she had scolded Leah about James. And she had been furious then. A shiver coursed up Leah's spine. Over Madame's shoulder she could see the small crowd that had gathered. Leah's eyes met Pam's. The curious, expectant look on her face made Leah feel sick. But she wasn't going to back down.

"If you don't apologize right now for your rude, uncalled-for behavior," Madame's voice bellowed threateningly, "you are to leave here at once. You will not take part in tonight's—or any other night's—performance here. And you are to see me in my office first thing tomorrow."

As if from a great distance, Leah heard herself answer loud and clear. "I will *never* talk to that woman again. So I guess I'll just get out of here now."

She spun around, marched past Madame, and bumped right into Lynne Vreeland. She was wearing her beautiful pink tutu from act one and she had a small tiara perched upon her head. "Leah?" she said in a bewildered voice.

Leah glared at her a moment, then pushed by.

"What's gotten into that girl?" Madame's voice rang out down the hall after her.

"Wait—" Lynne Vreeland cried. Leah continued down the hall without turning around. A moment later the ballerina had caught up with her. Leah walked even faster. Lynne Vreeland matched her angry stride.

"Leave me alone!" Leah shouted over her shoulder as she began to run. The ballerina kept pace with her. She refused to be put off so easily.

"What's the meaning of this?" Her voice was like ice. She grabbed Leah's arm and held her hard, forcing her to face her.

"Let me go!" Leah cried, staring right back into the flashing eyes.

She kept her grip on Leah and steered her down another corridor. She pushed open the door to a dressing room and led Leah inside.

Closing the door behind her, she leaned against it, crossing her arms in front of her, barring Leah's way.

"What's going on here?"

Leah didn't answer. She deliberately turned her head and began looking around the room. Suddenly she realized it was Lynne's dressing room. Vases of flowers covered every surface. A pair of familiar leather pants hung carelessly over a chair. The dressing table was littered with tubes of makeup and jars of greasepaint. A pink rabbit's foot dangled from the frame of a photograph. Leah frowned when she saw it was a recent picture of Lynne Vreeland with a handsome man. From the way they were standing, heads close, arms around each other's waists, Leah could tell he was her boyfriend. She thought of Kay's father and her fists clenched.

"I think I deserve an explanation," Lynne Vreeland said, taking a few cautious steps away from the door.

"Why?" Leah asked sharply.

"Because yesterday we seemed to be friends. I haven't seen you since then. I haven't talked to you since then. And you obviously—are—" She broke off and moistened her lips, carefully considering her words. "You're angry, Leah." Her voice was gentle, slightly coaxing. "What have I done?"

"You lied." The answer sprang to Leah's lips before she had time to think about it.

"I lied?" She looked astonished, but said nothing for a moment. Then she asked cautiously, "About what, may I ask?"

Leah shrugged. Was it really a lie she had told?

No, it was more than that. "It wasn't exactly a lie," Leah stated flatly, staring down at her hands. They looked very pale against the rosy fabric of her costume. "I think it's more that you're a—a hypocrite." Leah's voice shook. "Yes, that's the right word. Someone who pretends to be what she is not."

"You have no right to say that!" Lynne Vreeland's voice was low and furious.

"I do, too," Leah retorted, her voice rising. The knot inside her chest was growing tighter. She began to feel as if she were about to explode. "I know *all* about you, Miss Vreeland. You and your mistake!"

"What are you talking about?" Lynne Vreeland looked as if someone had punched her in the stomach. An angry flush spread up her chest and neck.

"I'm talking about Kay!" The words shot out of Leah like a bullet.

"Kay?"

Leah lost all control, and burst out with a sob, "Kay Larkin, your daughter!"

Blinded by tears, she couldn't look at Lynne Vreeland anymore. The words spilled out of her in a torrent. "Kay's one of my best friends. She's a student here! She told me all about you last night," Leah shouted. She looked accusingly at Lynne.

Beneath her heavy stage makeup, Lynne Vreeland turned white. She stared at Leah in disbelief and slumped back against the wall. "Kay Larkin?" she asked in a hushed voice.

Something awful and vicious was on the tip of Leah's tongue, but when she saw the tragic expression in Lynne's eyes, she lost her voice. Lynne looked, at that moment, exactly as Kay had looked the night before. All Leah could do was nod. Her heart was pounding so fast she thought she would faint. What had she done?

"She's a student here? She's become a dancer?" Lynne was breathing deeply, unevenly.

She straightened up and with an absent gesture smoothed down the rumpled tulle of her skirt. A moment later she reached behind her back and unzipped the bodice. "Take me to her, Leah," Lynne whispered. She left her costume lying in a heap in the middle of the floor. She pulled on a pair of gray sweat pants and yanked off her tiara. A thick black sweater went over her head. She took off her pointe shoes and slipped into a pair of badly scuffed flats. "Take me to her," she said again, this time in a loud, firm voice.

"I—I can't," Leah stammered. "I promised—I promised not to tell anyone, and now—" Leah turned away from Lynne, conscious only of the fact that she had betrayed her dear friend.

"You did the right thing, Leah. Kay will understand that." Lynne's voice shook with emotion. She didn't sound angry, though. She sounded very sure, and even grateful as she took Leah's arm.

Leah looked up, her eyes full of questions.

"Take off your costume. Here, you can borrow these." She reached into the closet and handed Leah a pair of jeans and a baggy shirt.

"Lynne, what's going on in there?"

At the sound of Madame Preston's voice Leah looked at Lynne, terrified. Lynne put a finger to her lips. She cleared her throat and said in a calm voice, "I'll be back with Leah in a little while. Everything's okay. We just have some business to take care of. I'll be back in time for my entrance in act one."

After Madame's footsteps faded, Lynne cautiously opened the door and waited for Leah to follow her. Outside on the street, although it was raining, Lynne put on sunglasses and hailed a cab. Before they climbed in, she held Leah back and said, "I understand why you're upset with me, Leah, but you don't know the whole story. I was young then. I didn't realize what I was doing. I'd give anything to take back what I did, to make things different now."

Exhausted from her outbursts, Leah couldn't say a thing. She wondered the whole way to the boardinghouse if Lynne really meant what she said. If she had a chance to start over again, would she really give up her career for Kay?

Leah lifted the steaming mug of tea to her lips, but her hands were shaking so badly she had to put it down before she could take a sip. She kept picturing Kay's face when Mrs. Hanson called her down to the parlor. Kay had looked at Lynne and then at Leah with such total shock that Leah found herself wishing the San Andreas fault would open up and swallow her. She had never seen anyone look so betrayed and frightened in all her life.

Mrs. Hanson poured a cup of tea for herself and drew her chair up close to Leah's at the kitchen table. "I have no idea what's going on here, Leah, and believe me, I don't intend to betray any confidences, but I will have to make some kind of explanation to Madame Preston. She already called while you were on your way over and I know she is going to have a lot of questions."

Leah met Mrs. Hanson's eyes. They were the same shade of gray as her sister's, but they had flecks of gold in them and their expression was softer.

Mrs. Hanson folded her hands in her ample lap and studied her nails. "I want you to feel free to tell me whatever you want, dear. You need someone to trust around here. And don't worry, we don't have to tell Madame Preston everything. We will have to come up with some excuse, but I think we can find a way to bend the truth."

"I don't want to bend the truth. I don't want to lie. I'm just so confused. I promised Kay I wouldn't tell anyone her secret, and now look what I've done. What's going to happen now?" Leah cried out.

"Go on," Mrs. Hanson urged. She smoothed her flowered apron and discreetly looked away to make it easier for Leah to talk.

"Miss Vreeland is Kay's mother."

A gasp escaped from Mrs. Hanson's lips and then her look of puzzlement turned to one of comprehension. "Of course. That's who Kay reminds me of. And well, Miss Vreeland's child would be about Kay's age now," she mused.

"You knew she had a daughter?" Leah was flabbergasted.

"Well, it was no secret. In fact, fourteen or fifteen years ago it made headlines—in dance publications at least, and in some of the gossip columns. Lynne was just getting her first taste of international recognition, guesting with the European companies.

"She was such a young girl, and an unusually gifted dancer. The director of the company she was in at the time didn't approve of his ballerinas getting married, so she kept the wedding secret. Keeping a baby secret is another thing of course," she added.

Leah began to calm down. She picked up her tea and found her hands were steadier now. She leaned forward in her chair to listen more closely. Lynne's story suddenly seemed very important. Understanding Lynne, Leah realized, might help her understand herself better.

Settling back in her chair, Mrs. Hanson went on. "He fired her—or threatened to. I don't remember which. Alicia probably still remembers the details. Anyway, she left and had the baby, but after a few months she knew that she still had to dance. I guess she thought she had to make a decision between the two."

Mrs. Hanson paused and looked out the window at the rain. It was falling heavily now and the wind was rattling the shutters. "I guess everyone has different feelings about this sort of thing. Lynne probably didn't have to make that choice. It must have been hard on her. Who would ever have believed that her daughter would turn out to be as talented as she is? But I can understand why Kay would want to keep that kind of family background under her hat at a school like this. Look at how the other girls treat Alexandra because of her famous dancer parents. I am a bit surprised Madame never mentioned it to me, though."

"Madame doesn't know," Leah said quietly. She looked up at Mrs. Hanson and spoke slowly, trying to explain how awful things had been for Kay. "Kay never told anyone, ever," Leah said. "Until last night. She had mentioned her father had been divorced, but she never said her natural mother was a dancer."

Mrs. Hanson shook her head. "It must have been very difficult for her, too." She paused and looked at Leah. "And how did you get caught in the middle of all this?"

Leah closed her eyes for a moment and pressed her palms to her forehead. Lowering her hands, she said, "Miss Vreeland asked me to lunch yesterday and I went. I was so excited about it, and I didn't want Kay to feel left out of things so I got her an autographed picture. Kay blew up when I gave it to her. Her reaction didn't make any sense." Leah went on to tell Mrs. Hanson about her talk with Kay.

"I felt angry myself. I couldn't understand how anyone could do such a thing. Just up and leave a baby and a nice husband because of her dancing. I didn't want to believe a person had to do that to be great. I don't want to believe it now." Leah's voice sank very low and tears welled up in her eyes. "She told me all these wonderful things about dance, about how having a career was worth all the mistakes you might make along the way, how if she had a chance she'd say the same thing to her own daughter ..." Leah's voice trailed off and she dried her eyes.

It occurred to her now that Lynne Vreeland hadn't lied at all. She hadn't said she had a daughter, but she had never said she didn't either. Suddenly what Lynne had done didn't seem so awful. A lot of people had gotten hurt: Kay, her father, but Lynne, too. These were the kinds of choices a person had to make when they decided to become a dancer. Even her old teacher, Miss Greene, had talked about giving up everything for dance. Leah had never realized exactly what she had meant until now.

Mrs. Hanson seemed to be reading her mind. She began answering the question forming on Leah's lips before Leah even said a word.

"Believe me, Leah, whatever Lynne did, she had to do. Don't be too hard on her."

"I—I—think I understand a little better now why she did it. From what you say, it makes more sense. It just frightens me, knowing that to do what I love doing best means giving up so much." Tears started spilling down her cheeks again.

Mrs. Hanson didn't answer. She gathered the weeping Leah in her arms and let her cry. A few seconds later a sound at the kitchen door made them spring apart.

Kay and Lynne were standing in the doorway, a definite distance between them. Kay had obviously been crying and Leah was afraid to meet her eyes. Lynne's eyes were masked by her sunglasses as usual, but streaks of mascara on her cheeks showed she had been crying, too.

"It's okay, Leah," Kay said quietly. "I think this worked out for the best. We're going to get to know each other now, aren't we?" Anger still lurked in the corners of her face and her eyes had a hurt look about them, but there was a note of hope in her voice that made Leah smile.

"I think so," Lynne said, sounding a little unsure of herself. She shoved her glasses up on her head and blew her nose loudly. It was a very unglamorous, very unstarlike, very human gesture, and Leah's heart leapt to see it. Lynne looked radiantly happy, the way she looked, Leah thought, when she danced.

Chapter 12

Leah gathered the full skirt of her rose-colored gown in her hands and tiptoed behind the backdrop. Two technicians looked up from their mugs of coffee, and one of them winked at her. "Break a leg!" he said in a hearty voice.

Leah smiled but continued to look for Kay. She had left her a note in the corps dressing room to meet her backstage before the performance. Leah finally found her, sitting on top of a pile of sandbags with her arms around her knees, looking very vulnerable. She was dressed in the same jeans and red cotton sweater she had been wearing earlier that afternoon. She had returned to the theater with Leah and Lynne in a cab and apparently hadn't gotten a chance to go back and change.

As soon as they were inside the stage door, Kay had approached Madame before even Lynne could intercede. "What happened today was all my fault," she had said in a brave voice. "Don't blame Leah. I don't want her to get into any more trouble." At the time, Leah wasn't sure whether to punch her or hug her. Now she just wanted to sit next to her friend and let her talk.

"Did you have dinner together?"

Kay didn't answer right away. She gazed up at Leah and nodded her approval. "You look very beautiful tonight, Leah. I love your costume. It makes me wish I hadn't been such an idiot about all this. It must be fun walking around in such an exotic outfit. And that wig!" She stifled a giggle.

"Madame said you could still—"

Kay interrupted Leah quickly. "I don't want to. I want to see—my mother—" The word sounded funny on her tongue and Kay tried it again. This time it sounded more natural. "I want to see my real mom dance for the first time from up front. She got me a complimentary seat in the orchestra center. The best seat in the house, she said." A note of pride entered Kay's voice.

"I did want to apologize," Leah started to say.

Kay cut her off again. "No, Leah. It wasn't your fault. You were upset about her, too. Of course, I don't know if I'll tell you *all* my secrets from here on in ..."

Leah bowed her head. She deserved it. True friends didn't betray friends. Then Kay punched her arm playfully.

"You dope. Of course I'll tell you everything." Kay grinned, delighted she had fooled Leah. Then her face grew serious. "You did me the best favor anyone in the world has ever done for me. You introduced me to my own mother. I owe you a lot for that."

Leah reached over and hugged her friend. Her thick makeup rubbed off on Kay's chest.

"Yuk!" Kay protested, wiping the greasepaint

off her chin. "Mom took me to dinner, but we didn't eat, either one of us. I was able to talk to her some—about how I felt—feel." She looked down at her hands. They were clenched into two tight fists and her knuckles were white. Then she looked at Leah again. "It's not as though everything's fine yet," she said, her voice trembling slightly. "I've been upset a long time, and so has she. I hurt her, too, by never answering her letters, by refusing to see her. I hadn't thought about that before." Kay hugged her knees and confessed, "I didn't think parents could get hurt the way kids can." She bit her lip and when she looked back at Leah, tears darkened her eyes. With a brusque gesture she wiped them away. "So I guess it's going to take time to get over all the pain we've caused each other. But I'm definitely going to start seeing her on a more regular basis. I want to get to know her. She's a pretty interesting person."

"And what about school? What about your own dancing?" Leah asked. She hid her fingers under her long skirt and crossed them, hoping for the best.

"I guess I'll stick around awhile," Kay said, looking sheepish. "After all, it's in my blood."

"Oh, Kay!" Leah clapped her hands and jumped up. She pulled Kay to her feet and spun her around. Leah's full skirt caught on a piece of scenery, and Kay screeched for her to stop. "You're going to bring the house down if you're not careful," Kay joked, her eyes shining.

"Ten minutes until curtain!" Andrew's voice rang out. Leah got a nervous fluttery feeling in her stomach.

"Go on." Kay pushed her over toward the wings.

"I've got to get out front. I can't walk in late to the best seat in the house on opening night dressed like this."

Leah hugged her again then held her friend at arm's length. Kay regarded Leah a moment and said very quietly, "It's been a crazy week." She ran her fingers through her hair. It was hanging down and loose and she looked very much like her mother. "But I'm glad the bad part is over." Kay turned to go, then added, "Oh, and Leah, I talked to Madame. She called school and set up an appointment for me with the counselor. You know what else she said?" Kay's voice dropped to a conspiratorial whisper. "She said all this will make me a better dancer someday. I don't know what she meant by that."

"Five minutes until curtain. Clear the stage, please."

Kay blew a kiss to Leah and sped down the hall toward the auditorium door. Leah stood quietly and watched her disappear, her words still ringing in Leah's ears. ". . . All this will make me a better dancer someday."

"I know what she meant, Kay," Leah whispered after her as Wayne ran up in his plumed hat. Facing whatever life would bring her would make her a better dancer. Leah vowed to remember Madame's words as she put her hand gracefully on her partner's arm and stepped into position in the wings. Maybe everything she went through because of Kay had helped shape Lynne Vreeland into a truly great dramatic star.

Leah looked up. Across the broad expanse of empty stage she spotted Lynne. She was dressed in her act one tutu, a blue sequined sweater over the bodice, her ugly moth-eaten leg warmers bunched up around her ankles as she chatted with one of her turbaned cavaliers.

She lifted her eyes for a moment and caught Leah's glance. Then Lynne inclined her head and stepped into a gracious bow, the sides of her tutu brushing the dusty stage sets. She sank to one knee in a silent thank-you. The star's generous gesture brought tears to Leah's eyes just as the cue for her entrance rang out. With her arm resting lightly on Wayne's, Leah stepped onto the Opera House stage in front of a paying audience for the very first time. And at that moment she knew that in the end, whatever turns her life would take, to be a dancer was definitely worth it.

Glossary

Adagio. Slow tempo dance steps; essential to sustaining controlled body line. When dancing with a partner, the term refers to support of ballerina.

Allegro. Quick, lively dance step.

Arabesque. Dancer stands on one leg and extends the other leg straight back while holding the arms in graceful positions.

Assemblé. A jump in which the two feet are brought together in the air before the dancer lands on the ground in fifth position.

Ballon. Illusion of suspending in air.

Barre. The wooden bar along the wall of every ballet studio. Work at the barre makes up the first part of ballet class.

Battement. Throwing the leg as high as possible into the air to the front, the side, or the back. Several variations.

Bourrée. Small, quick steps usually done on toes. Many variations.

Brisé. A jump off one foot in which the legs are beaten together in the air.

Centre work. The main part of practice; performing steps on the floor after barre work.

Chaîné. A series of short, usually fast turns on pointe by which a dancer moves across the stage.

Corps de ballet. Any and all members of the ballet who are not soloists.

Dégagé. Extension with toe pointed in preparation for a ballet step.

Developpé. The slow raising and unfolding of one leg until it is high in the air (usually done in pas de deux, or with support of barre or partner).

Echappé. A movement in which the dancer springs up from fifth position onto pointe in second position. Also a jump.

Fouetté. A step in which the dancer is on one leg and uses the other leg in a sort of whipping movement to help the body turn.

Jeté. A jump from one foot onto the other in

which the working leg appears to be thrown in the air.

Mazurka. A Polish national dance.

Pas de deux. Dance for two dancers. ("Pas de trois" means dance for three dancers, and so on.)

Piqué. Direct step onto pointe without bending the knee of the working leg.

Plié. With feet and legs turned out, a movement by which the dancer bends both knees outward over the toes, leaving the heels on the ground.

   Demi plié. Bending the knees as far as possible leaving the heels on the floor.

   Grand plié. Bending knees all the way down letting the heels come off the floor (except in second position).

Pointe work. Exercises performed in pointe (toe) shoes.

Port de bras. Position of the dancer's arms.

Positions. There are five basic positions of the feet and arms that all ballet dancers must learn.

Retiré. Drawing the toe of one foot to the opposite knee.

Tendu. Stretching or holding a certain position or movement.

Tour en l'air. A spectacular jump in which the dancer leaps directly upward and turns one, two, or three times before landing.

Here's a look at what's ahead in CHANGING PARTNERS, the fourth book in Fawcett's "Satin Slippers" series for GIRLS ONLY.

"I guess you and I can survive another audition," Leah tried to sound cheerful as she carefully positioned herself away from Alex's long legs and faced the barre for some plies.

"The chance of dancing with Andrei Levintoff in a gala—with reporters and critics, Stephenson, makes this something more than 'another audition,'" Alexandra replied sharply. Leah bit her lip. Of course Alex would feel like that, considering how her heart was set on Andrei. Alex saw Leah's reflection in the mirror, and her expression softened slightly. "But I'd rather have you get it than that—that—" Alex gave up trying to compare Pam to anything worth mentioning.

It was a backhanded compliment, but Leah knew it was the best Alex could do—she was a proud girl who knew she was the best dancer currently enrolled in the school, besides Leah. But Leah wasn't quite up to Alex's level yet: she was two years younger, without the performing experience or the stamina that Alex possessed. No one at SFBA could possibly imagine anyone but Alex getting the part, and Leah knew that Alex would feel humiliated if she didn't. For Alex, this was a very important gala—she would probably leave the school next year, and most likely would have no trouble getting into a major company. Yet, even with her considerable talent, the honor of dancing with Andrei, as well as any positive reviews, would be very helpful to her career right now. Leah wondered aloud, "Why is Pam here?"

Alex again met her glance in the mirror and shrugged her shoulders. "Beats me!" A moment later Andrei walked in, followed by two other boys from the school. Don Bryson, Pamela's latest partner, was one of them. He was older than Alex, and Leah didn't know him well. He lived in the Bay Area in his own apartment and was already auditioning for companies.

The other boy, Michael Litvak, walked right up to Leah. He was a nervous sixteen-year-old with a rangy build who had been her partner before she was paired up with James. After James's accident, Michael and Leah were assigned to work together again.

"So today we learn the pas de deux from *La Bayadere.* "The ballet that is danced with a scarf." Michael cracked his knuckles. Leah sometimes felt sorry for her tall skinny partner. He was a talented dancer who just needed a few years to fill out and get stronger. Leah had learned the only way to deal with him was to play down his fears. When they danced together she forced herself to put aside her own trepidation and throw herself at him before he had a chance to worry that he might drop her. His lifts had improved greatly over the past month or so and people were beginning to talk about how well they moved together. Leah felt secretly pleased to know Michael's improvement as a partner was due mainly to her.

"This should be fun," she said forcing herself to smile as she experimented with a couple of pose turns, her hands on her hips. She couldn't help but wonder why Andrei was bothering to teach them the pas de deux, since Madame had announced that he would partner the chosen girl in a new piece created for the occasion.

"Okay, everyone," Andrei said. All conversation stopped. Leah faced him and blushed a little when his glance seemed to linger on her for a moment. Today she had dressed with particular care. She was wearing her favorite pair of turquoise stud earrings, that played up the blue of her large eyes. Her black tank top leotard was the slinky kind that clung to every curve. Leah was slender but had a nice figure, and she couldn't help but wonder if Andrei had noticed. Then she remembered Alex. She bit her lip and scolded herself for thinking of Andrei like that. *Professional competition is one thing, competing over Andrei is something else,* she repeated to herself over and over.

"Today," Andrei continued, "you probably wonder what all these people are doing here." Andrei's eyes seemed to settle on Alex a ltitle, and Leah caught the barest hint of a smile on his lips. "Well, I think you boys can relax a little. None of you will have the chance to be my partner."

Everyone in the room cracked up and some of the tension was broken.

"But I have chosen you three girls out of all the others, because you are all about the right size."

Leah's face fell even though she knew he had a point—whoever danced with Andrei couldn't be too tall. Alex was taller than Leah but still short enough to work with a guy Andrei's size. Pam was Leah's height but quite a bit heavier. Leah wondered if he could lift her, then remembered Pam's spectacular jump. A good jump helped during a lift. Besides, Andrei's arms looked very muscular.

"Because I watched you very carefully in the repertory class yesterday, I see you all are very strong dancers."

Leah's hopes soared just a little. At least being five-foot-four wasn't the only reason she was there.

"So today I work with all of you. I understand none of you have danced the pas de deux from *La Bayadere* before, and I am sure you look forward to learning it."

To the right of Leah, Alex groaned.

Andrei heard her and laughed. "I just want to see how well we work together on this. I will see what the strength is of each girl. Though I am sure each one will inspire me to choreograph the new ballet, no?"

Leah just nodded. Once upon a time picturing herself as inspiring the great Andrei Levintoff might have struck her as silly. Now it was frighteningly real.

ABOUT THE AUTHOR

Elizabeth Bernard has had a life-long passion for dance. Her interest and background in ballet is wide and various and has led to many friendships and acquaintances in the ballet and dance world. Through these connections she has had the opportunity to witness first-hand a behind-the-scenes world of dance seldom seen by non-dancers. She is familiar with the stuff of ballet life: the artistry, the dedication, the fierce competition, the heartaches, the pains, and the disappointments. She is the author of over a dozen books for young adults, including titles in the bestselling COUPLES series, published by Scholastic, and the SISTERS series, published by Fawcett.